PEDDLAR'S SCAR

PEDDLAR'S SCAR
By
JAMES RIGBY

REWORD PUBLISHERS

2003

Published by
REWORD PUBLISHERS
3 Syddal Crescent
Bramhall
Cheshire SK7 1HS
www.reword.co.uk

© James Rigby 2003

ISBN 0 9536743 7 1

Printed and bound by
GOPSONS PAPERS LTD
INDIA

This book is dedicate to

My Wife Gwen
and to the memory of my two Daughters
Tracey Jane and Heather Nancy
who died in a car accident fifteen years ago
and
to freemasonry for whom
The friendship and brotherhood
will always be a source of inspiration.

ABOUT THE AUTHOR

James Rigby was born on Walney Island in May 1939 and educated at Vickerstown School and Walney Secondary Modern. He served his apprenticeship with Vickers Engineering as a fitter and turner, then, following a three-year break in the Merchant Marines, returned as an engineering inspector. It was whilst working in Jersey as a diesel engineer for an International company, that he met his future wife Gwendoline. His earlier interests were rifle-shooting, being a protégé of his uncle, later taking up amateur operatics in Barrow.

Their first daughter Tracey was born on the Island whilst Jim was on National Service in Aden, and consequently missed the first five months of her life. His second daughter was born in Preston Lancashire whilst he was working as a Service manager for an international chemical engineering manufacturer, a career that took him to many parts of Europe.

In 1988 both his daughters died in a car crash near his village of Holmes Chapel in Cheshire, a tragedy that lead to Jim deeply involving himself in Freemasonry. He has had several poems published and has written articles for a local newspaper on the escapades of three World War II submarines that had been built at Barrow.

Having served as a Borough Councillor for five years, Jim and his wife of almost forty-years will soon be retiring back to Jersey, but he still intends to carry on writing.

PEDDLAR'S SCAR
By
JAMES RIGBY

CHAPTER ONE

The 7th.of May 1941. At 4.45pm Norman 'Nobby' Pearce had finished winding the last of the thirty-two antique clocks. Pausing, he put on his overcoat as he had been doing every day for the past seven years when he joined the company.

'I'm off then Mr Richardson.'

'Right oh! Nobby, See you in the morning.'

Richardson's, in Dalton Road, were the oldest watchmakers and jewellers in Barrow, having retailed there for over forty years.

Going to the back of the building, he carefully checked his tyres and tested his brakes. His beloved bicycle, a Hercules Kestrel with Archer gears, black and gold frames and two leather panniers on the back, had cost him five-pounds the year before when he joined Barrow Wheelers Cycling Club.

'With enough tools to build a submarine,' his wife remarked with humour.

He rang his bell before mounting, for Nobby was in a hurry. He had five minutes to get down to Schnieder Square, cross the tramlines over Michaelson Bridge, and pass the main gates of Vickers-Armstrong and Maxim before the five o'clock siren went off. Then some two thousand workmen would come running, riding or walking through the first of the eight main gates. They had no mercy on passers by in the rush to get home and he would be taking his life in his hands if he got caught up in it.

He made it! Arriving at his home in Abercorn Street, he carefully parked his bike outside the back door and entered.

From upstairs his wife shouted, 'Is that you Norman?'

'Yes dear,' he replied.

'I'll be down in a minute.'

He eased the coat from his shoulders, hanging it in the lobby, an effort that required manoeuvring along carefully placed newspapers on the floor. Looking into the front parlour he picked up the letters awaiting him in a neat pile. Taking great care not to step into the sanctum sanctorum that was so immaculately kept for the privileged visitors, he turned and looked into the wall mirror and studied himself.

'Thirty four years of age, lightly balding, weighing about twelve stone, slightly overweight for his height of five foot seven. He opened his letters. One was from the Barrow and District Rifle League, where he was secretary and his wife, Violet, treasurer, informing him that he had won the Lancashire Masters Medal and the presentation would be at the Drill Hall in October. The others, also from the League, were the targets from last week's shoot, which required marking.

'Norman, take your boots off if you go in the parlour.'

'Yes dear.'

'I've laid out your uniform. What time are you on duty?'

'Midnight to four o'clock, dear.'

'Right, I'm coming down now. Your tea is ready.'

Walking through the living room into the kitchen he could already smell the aroma of his favourite dish, tripe and onions, with boiled potatoes. The potatoes were fresh from his allotment. After tea he was allowed to snooze in his armchair whilst his wife listened to the repeats of 'Workers Playtime' on the wireless. At ten o'clock she gently woke her husband up

'Come on Norman, time to get going.'

After washing and shaving in kitchen, he lit the storm lamp and went to the outside toilet, remembering to take several cuttings from the 'News of the World' to hang up. He lit the paraffin lamp to keep the chill out of the night air.

Returning to the house, he made his way upstairs to the where his uniform lay perfectly arranged on the bed. After dressing, he returned downstairs, again admiring himself in the mirror.

A smug look of satisfaction came over his face. 'Sergeant Norman Pearce. B Company Home Guard.' Pausing, he opened the lobby cupboard and took out his Lee-Enfield 303 rifle, his own property, not Government Issue. Tucking two clips of ammunition into his pocket he went back into the kitchen to collect his supper that his wife had his packed. After kissing her goodbye, he cycled off towards the Drill Hall. Passing number eight, Andover Street at the bottom of the hill he looked up at the rear bedroom. Rita Forshaw smiled down at him and winked.

'See you tomorrow Nobby,' she silently mouthed, blowing him a kiss.

On arriving at The Drill hall he reported to Company Sergeant Major William Waters, First County of Lancaster (Barrow Home Guard).

'Evening sir.'

'Evening Nobby,' replied the officer, responding to his salute.

'Gas works again. All right?'

'Yes sir.' Then, sighing, 'See you later.'

'Ok. Oh! Don't forget, Elliscales Quarry, Sunday morning. I want you to take the lads for live practice rounds.'

The evening was very quiet until two o'clock in the morning when the air-raid sirens went off over the town. It was exactly 3.19am when the first bombs started to fall. From the Gas works Nobby watched as the 150-foot tower crane exploded at its base, then he heard the sound of machine-gun firing in the distance. Emerging from the gloom the first of two German Bombers were flying at almost roof top level.

'Bastards!' he screamed, firing a shot at the dark grey object in the night sky.

Tom Cooke and Chris Fieldhouse, volunteer fire-watchers, opened their lunch packs as they sat on top of Number-one tower-crane high above Buccleugh Docks. From this vantage point they could see across Morecambe Bay estuary and the first flashes as bombs struck Liverpool.

'Do you reckon we'll get it tonight mate?' Chris asked Tom.

'Who knows? I'ts been quiet for the last month.'

'Its bound to be our turn again soon,' he replied pensively. Tom, had lost his house in Vernon street and was now lodging with Chris, whilst his wife and baby were staying with his mother- in-law.

They looked down at the Steamship 'Fishpool' in the dock below them, then across to Ramsden Dock, where two aircraft carriers were anchored, awaiting final fitments. Ahead of them, in Devonshire Dock, four submarines, floating like giant whales, which had recently been completed and were now awaiting commissioning. Vickers, being one of the largest armament naval dockyards in the country, employed some 15,000 men and women, incorporating boiler-shops, turbine-shops, marine-fittings, brass and steel foundries, gun shops and tanks, as well as industrial kilns. All were being manufactured at Barrow.

Across the docks stood the breweries and paper works. Half a mile up the road, the iron-ore works of Barrow, and, shadowing across Duddon estuary, the Millom Iron Works.

'Surprises me they have never come every night. All they have hit up to now are houses and churches.'

'They must be ruddy blind,' his mate scoffed ponderously.

Just then the air raid warnings started up.

'Me and my big mouth. Here they come.'

Across on Walney Island the Ack-Ack guns opened fire. The first bombs fell on the marshes at Biggar Bank. Then the first bomber was sighted, coming down the length of the docks. Chris and Tom were blown off their feet as, with an almighty flash, a missile struck the base of the tower. It seemed like an eternity, when, looking at each other in dumbstruck horror, the tower collapsed, sending them to the docks below, amongst the twisted metal girders. Then the second bomber came in from the direction of Piel Island, passing over Salthouse Road, Nelson Street, Howard Street, and Duke Street, shadowing St. Mary's Catholic Church. Two land mines floated down toward the granary, but did not explode.

Above the steel-works, one of the bombers was hit, veering off towards Walney Aerodrome where it was hit again by continued fire from the local shore-batteries. It was last seen in flames, heading towards the Welsh hills.

In the distance, over Askam Marshes, another bomber was hit. With smoke billowing from both engines it appeared to be heading directly for Blackcombe Mountain.

Some 30 minutes later when the 'all-clear' alarms had been sounded, the people of Barrow returned home from their shelters. As Bill Sykes said when he stepped out into the cold night air, 'What's Goering got against Newland Street? Vickers is only a hundred yards away.'

Muted laughter echoed after him.

Across on Walney Island, Fred Wright looked at his wife Winnie. 'That's it! We've evacuated Alan, Joan and Ken to Shap, but that's the last straw. You, the baby, Heather and David are off to Seathwaite to stay at Ray and Margaret's farm till all this ruddy mess is sorted out.'

'I'm certainly not!' she retorted, stamping her feet as she folded her arms under her ample bosom. 'Young Winnie is staying with me, but Heather and David can go. Heather can help on the farm; she's nearly sixteen and can look after her brother. I'm not leaving you here on your own, and until we get a house of our own, my brother Jim, and Nancy will look after us.'

'Well all right then,' he conceded. 'Tomorrow you check with the school and I'll write to Ray and Margaret.

'You'd better tell the kids, I don't think they will to be too unhappy. They enjoyed farming in the Lake District last year.'

CHAPTER TWO

Major Adolph (Bart) Bauer sat in the rear of the Junkers 87 bomber, cursing his superiors for the way they had chosen to get him into England. 'Of all the damned idiotic ideas to drop me on a bombing raid. Why not by Submarine? I am more likely to be shot down between France and Liverpool than being sunk in the Irish Sea.'

Putting his curses to one side, he went over his brief again. To penetrate the dockyards of Barrow; liase with their agent in the Lake District and, most importantly, find out if there is to be a meeting of allied Naval commanders. If so, find out where is it to be located? The agent will arrange suitable cover for you. You will be parachuted over the English fells and make your way to the village of Broughton. Seek out the local trade shop for joinery, plumbing and decorating, and ask for Niall O'Leary.

'Simply bloody simple. Land in the middle of nowhere, walk into a village as a stranger, and expect to mingle.'

Aged twenty-four, Bauer had been educated at Sheffield where his father and mother had lived for many years. They had been forced back to Germany in 1936 as the Spanish civil war was causing a lot of friction amongst the English. He had visited parts of the Lake District as a boy, boating on Windermere Lake and fishing along the river Lune at a place called Tebay, It all seemed a lifetime away now.

'Breaking away from the main Squadron now,' announced the pilot over the intercom. The Squadron consisted of eight bombers. Six were to attack the port of Liverpool first and then move on to Barrow. The two others were to head directly for Barrow via Morecambe Bay, then, after bombing the docks, were to turn east up the Eskdale valley and drop their passenger before rejoining the squadron.

'Walney Island coming up. Bomb doors opening,' Unterofficer Max Riss shouted out. 'Target ahead. One cargo-ship. Steady. Bomb gone.' The bomb whistled down, striking the base of one of the towers, causing it to collapse.

'Steady, steel works coming...' He did not finish his words. Unknown to him it was a 303 bullet that entered his jaw, exiting through the back of his head, killing him instantly. At the same time the plane was hit by Ack-Ack and the port engine caught fire.

'The Mountain! Shiesse, the Mountain! Jesus Christ!' The pilot yelled, forcing back the joy-stick with all his might in order to gain height as Blackcombe loomed ahead. With one engine screaming and the other now burning fiercely as they skimmed along the mountain side.

'We need more height. Christ! Max is dead,' yelled the navigator. 'We still have one bomb on board.'

'Well fucking get back there and release it, Now! Now! Now!'

As they swooped up the valley, Bauer made his way to the bomb-aimer's chair and pressed the release button. They were so close to the ground that he heard the blast behind them.

'Make height. For god's sake, make height.'

As they slowly gained altitude the starboard engine stopped.

'Were going in! Brace yourselves.'

'There is only us two left. Bauer has jumped. We' re going in. Oh! Christ.'

Suddenly and inevitably they hit the side of the mountain. The bottom of the plane struck the loose shale, and for two hundred yards they skidded, side on. And then they stopped.

Through the port window the pilot looked out. His hands were shaking, his heart was pounding. 'Oh! My God, we are alive.'

He stared out of the starboard window and below him could see a forest about one hundred and fifty feet down the embankment.

'What the hell?'

There was a rumbling and then they felt the plane move as the avalanche of loose shale and slate started to shove the plane down the mountain side.

'Oh! Christ! Here we go again. Brace yourself Bart.'

CHAPTER THREE

Simon Hughlock, MP. for Workington and Whitehaven, poured a glass of wine out for his wife Leslie and daughter-in-law Jane.

'To you Jane, to Mark, and especially the baby,' he toasted. 'When is it due?' pointing at the roundness of her stomach.

'Four months and twenty seven days to be exact,' she laughed.

Jane Hughlock was very pretty, with short curly blonde hair and petite figure, her bubbly personality adhered her to every one she met.

'So Jane! When do you hope to see Mark next?' her father in-law asked politely.

'Well, it was to be a surprise,' she answered, 'but I phoned a friend of mine who works in the naval operations department in Portsmouth, and I gather his ship will be arriving tomorrow. I' m hoping he can get leave to visit us here.'

'Jane that's terrific. It must be nearly five months since you and he were here last.'

'Simon, please. My dear husband, you are embarrassing the girl,' complained his wife, tut-tutting.

'What? Oh I didn' t mean,' Simon spluttered. 'Well at least something came out of it,' he continued, coyly looking over his spectacles.

Jane smiled shyly. She had been in love with Mark Hughlock since she was six years old, when they both went to school in Broughton. They were always together, playing by the Gypsy caravan and listening to the stories of Mara O' Leary. Mara, whose name came from the Westmoreland word for a miner's mate, broke his heart was when Jane married Mark. His son Niall, whom they had always called by his nickname 'Peddlar', had also been madly in love with Jane, though neither she nor Mark was aware of it, at least until Mark asked him to be his Best-man. Celebrating at the King's Head Inn at Broughton, Peddlar drank too much ale and poured his heart out with a vengeance. As a result they fought for over an hour until Mark managed to beat him. Peddlar went back to the caravan, packed his few belongings and left the district.

Mara lived in his beloved caravan and worked on Simon Hughlock's Estate as gamekeeper and water-bailiff. Tragedy had struck his family twenty-two years earlier when he first came to the valley. His wife and four daughters died as the result of eating poisonous mushrooms, leaving him with a year old son to bring up. Over the years he became an expert in all rural activities and could name every species of fauna and flora.

The old man had been mentor to all three of them for so many years, and Jane had promised to visit him with the latest news of Mark, and his naval career to date. It was just gone three in the morning when the household was woken by the air-raid siren from Millom Iron works, across the valley. Jane came downstairs to find Simon and Leslie in the kitchen, drinking cups of tea. 'Looks like Barrow or the Iron Works may be in for it. I'm surprised they haven't tried to bomb all along the West Coast yet.'

From out of the Night sky they heard the sound of a plane, its engines screaming for all they were worth. As the noise got nearer, Simon got up from the kitchen table to look out of the conservatory window.

'Well, well, look at this.'

Down in the valley they could see the outline of an aircraft, one of its wings ablaze. It was in direct line with the peaks of

Blackcombe, trying to gain altitude, when they saw the other wing catch fire.

'Dear, dear,' said Arthur's wife. 'Is it one of ours or theirs?'

They stood together staring into the night sky and, for some inexpressible reason, joined hands. That was when the bomb struck. The blast from the bomb was only superseded by the vibration of the aircraft as it flew over the caravan, bringing Mara from his bed and into the open air.

'Oh dear God, the house.' Pulling up his trousers he told Bella, his foxhound, to stay.

'What's that dad?' The voice came from the bedroom.

He shouted back. 'It's the house son, the house. Come quick, the old man and his wife are up there.'

They struggled up the long winding lane as flames from a wing of the house lit up the sky. Then, as suddenly has the flames appeared, they died out, leaving an ominous silence, with just the silhouette of the house outlined in the glow of the moon.

On reaching the Mansion they looked upon what was once the kitchen, a place where Mara and his son had spent many hours chatting and talking. Now there was nothing, absolutely nothing. As they stood there, Peddlar screamed. By his feet he saw the lovely face of Jane staring sightless into his.

'God, Oh God. Why her of all people?'

CHAPTER FOUR

It only seemed like seconds when Bauer hit the side of the fell. As soon as he pressed the bomb-aimer's button, he had opened the door and, glancing around, decided that if he was going to get killed he might as well chance the drop. Fortunately the parachute had opened almost immediately in the cold night air. The ground sloped at a steeply and he was lucky to miss the many boulders that were scattered around. He found himself sitting in a lay-by beside the roadside, rubbing his ankle and praying silently to the heavens. He opened his map, dawn was almost breaking and he was able to read it without a light. He appeared to be on Hard Knott Pass, a Roman road built to connect the port of Glannaventa, now called Ravenglass, with Ambleside via Wrynose pass, an ancient packhorse route to Carlisle and Hadrian's wall.

Estimating that he was about eight miles from Broughton by road, a journey that would take him the best part of the day to walk, the German was in the midst of packing the parachute when he heard the oncoming sound of a motorbike.

Police Sergeant Peter Thompson had left Carlisle at about one o'clock that morning, having visited an elderly aunt, the sister of his mother who had passed away a month earlier. He had arrived the day before from London, having been called into the Naval Intelligence office to carry out a special assignment. A meeting of chief naval personnel officers had been arranged at Ravenglass Castle in ten days time. Details of the meeting were expected to arrive by Naval courier at Broughton in a few days, by order of Sir Arthur Duckworth, the Naval Attaché at Ravenglass Castle.

Thompson had been ordered to take temporarily charge of Broughton police station, under the direction of Chief Superintendent Moses, and to investigate enemy radio transmissions that appeared to be coming from the south-west hills of the Lake District. He had been given permission to utilise, if necessary, any personnel from the Haverigg army camp.

As his 197 Francis-Barnet put-putted its way over the narrow pass, Thompson saw the lay-bye and pulled into it. Dismounting, he suddenly he felt a pain in his back, and as he looked down he saw blood appearing from his stomach. 'Rather strange,' he thought, 'that wasn't there before.' Turning, he saw through misting eyes, the grim face of a man in a flying-suit. He didn't know it, but he was dead before he hit the ground.

Bauer walked up to the body, and observing the youthful figure before him. 'He must be about my age,' he thought. He pulled the body behind a boulder at the edge of the wayside and loosely covered it, then opened the pannier on the bike. He could not believe his luck, for neatly packed inside he discovered a police uniform, complete with Sergeant's stripes, and an envelope containing some papers with instructions and contacts throughout the area.

CHAPTER FIVE

Lieutenant Commander Mark Hughloch huddled up on the rear seat of the Avro Anson aircraft, the noise of the engines increasing the numbness of his mind. Only days before, he and his crew had been celebrating a successful conclusion to their mission aboard the submarine 'H.M.S. Tipstaff' and were looking forward to some well-earned leave ashore.

However, he had been unexpectedly called to the Naval Commander's office and would never forget that look on the Staff Officers face.

'Sit down Mark. I won't beat around the bush, but there is no easy way to express what I'm about to tell you.'

There was a silence that seemed an age, and Mark could feel a heavy foreboding coming down on him. 'It's Jane isn't it? I told her to go to my parents in Lancashire. Well it is, isn't it? Come on spit it out.' Hysteria began to rise in him.

'Yes Mark, but I'm afraid it's a lot worse. Yesterday morning a German plane released a bomb over the Lake District. I'm afraid your father's house received a direct hit. I'm sorry son, but your father, mother, and Jane were killed instantly. God knows why better than we, but I can only assume the plane had been hit and was jettisoning its load. I have arranged with the Admiral for you to extend your leave indefinitely. There is a plane leaving Portsmouth in about two hours, taking dispatches to Barrow Shipyard. You should arrive at Walney aerodrome two hours after take off. I am so sorry, I knew your father very well and I'm sure the condolences of us all go with you. Ring me in a day or two to let me know where you are staying.

The drone of the aircraft engines changed, and Mark looked out of the window. They had left the Welsh hills behind them and crossed the Morecambe estuary. Below him he could see the South-End Lighthouse and Biggar Village and, to the right, the channel that separated Walney from Barrow Island.

Walney is shaped like a bent banana and is eleven miles long and about one mile wide at its widest point. It was the natural breakwater for one of the biggest shipyards in Great Britain. Fifty years earlier there were only about 250 people living there, but, with the mines closing in Cornwall, workers came to the Hematite iron-ore and lead mines sited around Barrow. The influx increased the population by some 50,000. In 1941 Walney aerodrome, sighted at the north end of the island, was a training ground for both pilots and a company of the WAAF's. In the middle of the island stood 'Vickerstown,' built by the Dockyard Engineering Company for its workers. The land across the narrow strip of water was dominated by the giant slag heap, grown from all the waste produced by the steel company. Each night the sky was illuminated by the miniature drag-trains hauling the molten slag to the top and dumping it into the channel.

Mark heard the sound of the landing wheels being lowered as they flew in just above roof top level, skimming over the Crown Inn. A few seconds later they landed. Crunch, crunch, a wait, crunch again. Then a mighty roar as the engines fought the thrust. Turning to face the small conning tower on the East Side of the airport, the engines picked up speed again for the short journey across to the hangars.

No formalities, everything arranged. A car already waiting to take him to Barrow Station. The driver offered a brief 'Good morning, sir,' then, after saluting, 'I'll take your luggage sir.'

And that was it. They drove out of the aerodrome, past the WAFF's billets down through the old-world village of North Scale and along the channel side. On the right he noticed the children playing in Vickerstown school, then, further on, they came to the new Jubilee Bridge that had been built to replace the cross channel ferry. Passing the sheds of Vickers Engineers, the deafening banging of machines in full motion could be heard, only dwarfed by the noise of the hammering in of wedges on the slipways, where two Cruisers were awaiting launching.

A mile further they reached Michaelson Road bridge, where, to his right, he saw the large crane lying in a tangled heap. A diver was in the dock looking for unexploded parachute-bombs, his companion in a rowing boat busily cranking the hand compressor. Travelling on they then came to the Town Hall with its towering clock facing all points: North, East, West, and South. Then along Duke Street to Ramsden Square and into Abbey Road, reputed to be the longest tree lined road in England.

The church and swimming baths had been reduced to rubble during the latest bombing raid and, as the car pulled up the station, he found the frontage and cafe had also been badly damaged.

Mark waited while the driver opened the door and took the luggage from him. Returning his salute, Mark walked into the station, showed his warrant to the station attendant, and walked onto the platform. On the southbound side were a few couples, mainly servicemen o returning to their units, saying their last farewells to wives and sweethearts.

The platform on his side was very quite, save for the two children sitting on a bench next to the Station-Masters office.

One, a boy of about seven years of age, was totally engrossed in a comic. He was wearing a school uniform, and a piece of string with a label attached, hung around his neck. The girl, some five-foot eight inches in height, appeared to be of around eighteen years of age. Her dark brown hair fell almost to her waist, the tightly fitted belt of the grey mackintosh that she wore amplifying the curves of her breasts. Mark shook his head and silently cursed himself, feeling ashamed that these thoughts should be in his mind at a time like this.

A woman, obviously their mother, came out if the station masters office, and, with a natural maternal care, gave them instructions. 'Now remember to get off at Foxfield. Your uncle will be there with the pony and trap to take you to the farm. And please be good while you are there, it will only be a short while until this silly war is over.'

Mark went across to the woman and said, 'excuse me, but I'm getting off at Foxfield myself, and with your permission I'll see they get off ok.'

'Well thank you sir. This is Heather and this is my son, David. I'm sure they will be no trouble.' Both she and her daughter gave a brief courtesy, when in the distance they heard the chugging of the steam train. Soon it emerged from the tunnel, smoke billowing from its stack. As it pulled to a halt, Mark helped the children into their compartment. The young girl smiled and thanked him. 'Even without makeup on her mouth was full and inviting,' he thought to himself, as he closed the door, at the same time pulling down the leather belt that released the window so that the children could say their goodbyes.

'Bye, bye, children,' their mother called, waving her handkerchief, then blowing her nose. 'Don't forget to write, we will come up and see you as soon as your dad can get time off.'

'All aboard!' The station Master stood along side the carriage, looked up and down the platform, blew his whistle and waved his flag. The train slowly picked up speed and left the station. The sound of wheels soon quickened on the tracks as they ran along the coast. A brief stop at Askam, then, with the sea to the left and the Lancashire fells looming up in the distance, they settled back for the short journey to Foxfield

Ray Morgan was already there. He had arrived half an hour before the train was due, eager for a quick pint at the local. He had brought his drink outside the pub and, looking along the coast line towards Askam, estimated that he had at least time for another pint before watching the train come over the viaduct.

Morgan was a tall man, some six feet three inches. He had always been a sheep farmer as had his father before him. He loved the fells, the fox-hunting, and beating the Hughlock estate for pheasant. His proudest moment came the month before, when he was made a freemason, recommended no less than by Simon Hughloch. Now they would meet once a month above the King Charles's Head inn.

'Hey up! Time for a quick one,' calling to the barmaid whilst observing the plume of steam in the distance.

CHAPTER SIX

Oberleutenant Hans Richter stood gazing up at the aircraft embedded in the slate and shale of the mountain side. In all his years of flying he had never considered the miracle of survival as he felt now. As he looked along the face of the mountain, there was no evidence at all of a crashed plane. He tried to visualise the angle at which he had struck the ground and decided that it was akin to belly flopping on a runway. The loose shale had absorbed the impact and now the plane was lying at a 45 degree angle, the starboard wing buried in bramble and bracken by the edge of a forest. As he pulled out a cigarette, he heard his Navigator Horst Stellmach call him.

'Captain, give us a hand here.'

He looked at the cigarette he had been about to light, put it back in the pack, and climbed back into the body of the plane.

Horst was endeavouring to lift the remains of their dead Comrade.

'Give us a hand with Max will you!' he implored. 'We'll have to bury him.'

As they laid him on the ground, Richter examined him and remarked, 'that's not a shrapnel wound, he's been shot.'

'Shot or not, he's dead. Let's bury him and get out of here,' said the pilot.

Managing to dig a shallow grave, they covered his body with soil. Then, using a larger piece of slate as a head stone, they engraved it with a knife:

Unterofficer Max Riss 1921 - 1941

Their excertions over, Richter took out his cigarette and lit it. 'Horst my little friend, the weather is good, the plane is as good as camouflaged, the forest is hiding us, but we don't know where we are. If Bauer survived the parachute jump he can't be too far away. He said he had an agent in a village called Broughton. We have local maps, and we have survival rations for a couple of days. This is a mountain, so there must be a river or stream nearby.'

Then, pausing for a moment, he continued. 'So this is what we will do. We will rest here for a few days, scout the area and get our bearings. We are hidden from planes and we will use a fire only at night. When we are sure no one is looking for us we will try and find Bauer, or board a neutral ship along the coast. The rest, well, we will adjust to as we go along'.

'Why don't we just surrender?' implored his Navigator. 'We are on an island, so how are we going to get anywhere in this god forsaken wilderness?'

'Come Horst; perhaps God has not forsaken us, but meantime, that's an order.'

Willie, slowly and with an insolent smirk, raised his arm in mock salute. 'Hiel Hitler.'

CHAPTER SEVEN

The train pulled into Foxfield, Mark opened the door of the carriage and got out. David handed him his luggage and jumped down, whilst Heather stood for a moment at the door, looking over Marks shoulder.

'There! There!' she exclaimed, 'there's Uncle Ray.'

She and David waved, then, turning to Mark, Heather gave a brief smile and curtsey and said, 'thank you sir for your help.'

Uncle Ray, who was standing by his pony and trap, gave Heather and David a welcoming hug. As he did so he became aware of Mark approaching him.

'Well bless my sole, its Master Mark. Aye! lad I'm so sorry about your family; your mother and father were very good to us and the young mistress - well its just too sad to describe.'

Mark, feeling a lump coming to his throat, knew instantly that this was something he had to come to terms with quickly. He was used to seeing comrades wounded and had seen a lot of deaths at sea. However this was as personal as it could get. 'Hello Mr. Morgan. Thanks for your condolences, and my regards to your wife when you get home. By the way if there is room in your trap could you drop me off at the *Kings Head* in Broughton. I'll leave my gear there and get a taxi to Seathwaite.'

'There are no taxies now in Broughton sir. Alf McEwan's gone off to the army and his Dad's too infirm to drive. I'll be happy to take you to your home if that's what you want. I understand that the house is in perfect condition, with the exception of....' He stopped himself. 'Ah! Well! You'll see for yourself.' Picking up the reins, he called 'Onward Mabel'

The horse trotted along the narrow road to Broughton, briefly stopping at the *Kings Head*. After checking into his room he rejoined the family again, lying back for the four miles or so to Seathwaite. As he did so he noticed a quaint sign across the road from the inn.

PAINTERS, DECORATORS, PLUMBERS.

It had been carved into a block of wood about two feet wide and five feet high in a corrugated fashion so that as you approached the sign from an angle the names changed.

Below the sign a green Francis-Barnet 197 motorbike was parked.

CHAPTER EIGHT

Baeur unpacked the police uniform and placed it on the dry grass. Removing his flying suit he opened Thompson's valise and dressed himself in the suit, white shirt and tie. The black shoes were a bit slack but he thought that when he had time he would fit some paper in the toes to stop them slipping. After packing away his own things into the valise, he tied it to the pannier of the motor bike, and, with several kicks of the starter-pedal, the bike roared into life, taking him down the pass.

The sun had now spread its golden tan over the fell side. The different shades of England's countryside always amazed him. A hare, startled by his engine, rushed across his path from the dry stone wall and into the bracken above him. Then, as he came round a sharp bend, he gasped at the panorama before him. Below, the village of Boot, and Dalegarth beyond. In the distance, which must have been some ten miles away, he could see a castle in the midst of woods, and beyond that, the sea. Fifteen minutes later he stopped to take a final look at the vision before him. There was still no one about, except some smoke from the few farms in the distance. He glanced up at a signpost which, although some attempt had been made to black out the name, he could make out 'Broughton, 4 miles'. He kicked the bike back into life and set off again. As he came down the fell-side the scenery began to change. Arriving at the Duddon bridge, a milestone on the edge of the road indicated Ulpha 2 miles, Seathwaite 4 miles, and Broughton 1 mile.

Approaching the village, he noticed the famous PAINTERS, DECORATORS, PLUMBERS sign. Driving round the corner, he came into the Village Square, in front of which stood the local police station, and, on the other side, a bank, a grocers, a mountain equipment shop and the 'Manor Arms'. Numerous men dressed in dark suits and carrying brief cases were milling around outside. He parked the bike in front of the police station, stood hesitating for a moment, took a deep breath and walked in.

There were two police constables in the station; one at the front- desk drinking a cup of tea, the other at the back, polishing his shoe's. PC John Bassett looked up over his cup and immediately placed it under the counter. 'Good morning Sergeant, weren't expecting you until this afternoon.'

'So it would appear Constable. Let's get the introductions over shall we. I am Station Sergeant Peter Thompson, on temporary assignment to the Broughton area. And you are?'

P.C. Basset sir and this is P.C. Wordsworth.'

'Any relation to the poet?'

'No Sarge.,' he said, smilingly wearily. He had heard it all before.

'Right then, show me were I go.'

'Your office is in here Sarge, and there is a telephone message from the Superintendent saying he wants to see you Friday morning here in the office at eleven thirty when he will brief you on the way to Ravenglass Castle.'

'Did he say what it's about?'

'No Serg., but there is a big buff envelope on your desk from him. Perhaps there's some information in it.'

'Thank you Basset. Make me a cup of that tea while I make myself at home.'

Bauer went into the office at the rear of the station, put his case and valise by the window, and sat down in the leather chair. 'So far, so good.'

P.C. Wordsworth entered. 'Lodgings have been arranged at the Manor Inn across the Square, Sarge, but I'd wait till this afternoon. There's a Masonic meeting on which should finish about eleven thirty.'

'Fine constable, I'll just read these papers and have a run around the village to get my bearings.' He opened the envelope before him. It was a plan map of Ravenglass castle, with instructions to accompany Chief Superintendent Moses there as soon as arrangements had been made. It welcomed him to Broughton, advising him to look for any strangers in the district, utilising Bassett's and Wordsworth's local knowledge. The letter went on to say that it had been one week since coded radio messages had been sent, and it was just possible that the perpetrator had left the area. No reference to the Friday meeting. Baeur assumed that was what the telephone message was about. He put the papers back in the envelope and went out into the front room.

'Right lads,' his Yorkshire background disguising his own Germanic tongue, 'I'll be back in an hour, and you can brief me on local people and what's going on here in Broughton.'

He walked out into the bright sunlit day. Sitting astride the motorbike he momentarily hesitated to consider his position. Up until now he had been extremely lucky, surviving the jump in the dark, and now this break to get inside an establishment. He realised that this was going to be a short-term assignment, for he did not know if Thopson was married, or who, if any one, may recognise him. What if there should be a telephone message from any of Thompson's friends in London? There were too many imponderables for his liking, but that was the name of the game, and his first task was to make contact with the agent O'Leary. He started the bike up and, as he swung around, he remembered that he was driving on the wrong side of the road. Stopping, he glanced up at two children standing at the grocers. 'Steady Bart,' he thought, 'remember where you are.' He turned the bike around again, and circled the square before riding down the hill to the joinery shop on the main street.

The door-bell rang as he entered. Paint tins, doors, and lengths of assorted timber lined one side. In the centre row, copper pipes, connections, and washers were laid out neat and orderly. whilst every available nook and cranny seemed to be filled with paint brushes, wall paper, yard brushes, and buckets. Bauer went to the counter; an old man wearing a brown smock peered over his glasses at him. Another man of about 24 years of age, some six-foot tall and well tanned, stood on a ladder behind the shopkeeper. Climbing down, he said cheerfully, 'Good morning Sergeant, your new here aren't you?'

'Yes, the names Thompson. I'm just making myself known to the shopkeepers. I'll be running the station for a few weeks as temporary replacement for your last officer.'

'I'm sure you will find it comfortable here,' said the old man, amicably. 'My name is Clark, Oliver Clark, and this is Niall O'Leary.'

Bauer looked at O'Leary, carefully weighing him up. 'You look is if you are a man of the mountains and streams.'

Despite his tan, O'Leary paled and took a step back. Quickly composing himself, he replied, 'The mountains and streams would make a man of even a stranger. Where are you staying, Sergeant?'

'At the moment,' replied Bauer, 'the Manor Inn across the square.' 'If you're going to be around this evening, perhaps you would like to join me for a drink. About eight, say?'

The young man nodded and turned to get back to his business. Bauer smiled and walked out.

CHAPTER NINE

It was about thirty minutes after they had set off that Mark Hughlock asked Morgan to stop the trap. 'Hold here Mr. Morgan, I think I'll walk the rest of the way.'

'Fine sir. Now if I can be of any assistance, well you know where we live, call any time. Onward Mabel.' Away went the pony at a steady trot.

Heather and David turned and waved as they carried on up the head of the valley before descending into the village of Seathwaite.

Mark looked at the lane to the left of him. It was about half a mile long and lined with rhododendrons in full bloom. Young rabbits were scurrying into the bushes, and the throaty call of a cock pheasant pierced sharply through the inner wood. He carried on up the rise until he came to a fork in the lane. To the right the track dipped down to open fields and a small copse, alongside which ran the Duddon river. Near to the copse he could see a Gypsy caravan, a dog laying in front of it, and a shire-horse tethered to an oak tree. A puff of smoke rose from the small chimney. Mark continued down the dry track, crossing a field, until he reached the oak. The Mare inquisitively came up to him and, as Mark stroked its head, said, 'Hello Hazel, it's nice to see you again old chum.' The horse grunted and stuck her head down towards Mark's pockets. 'Sorry old girl, I've nothing for you this time.' As he stood there he heard a soft wine at his feet, 'Bracken is it really you, it must be six years.'

At his feet was a brown and white foxhound, about eight years old, no collar but with a large scar from the left of its mouth to it ear. Mark recalled how he had found the dog on the fells, at the base of one of the quarries. It was just a pup then and was found in a sack along with four others. They were dead, but Bracken survived, although his jaw had been badly scarred when someone had thrown the sack over the quarry edge.

He fondled Brackens head and patted her on the back. As he was about to raise himself up, Mark heard a thud behind him. Imbedded in the tree, almost in line with his scalp, was a four-inch horseshoe that had been sharpened to a finely boned edge.

'You are loosing your touch Mara,' Mark called disapprovingly, without turning.

A laugh came from the caravan. 'Mark, son, I knew you would be back. Come in, come on in lad.'

As he entered, the years flooded back. He recalled how he, Jane, Niall, and Mara would sit there, stories ringing in their ears. At night they would talk and dream about the Romany ways, and how, when they grew up, they would travel the length and breadth of the Lake District as travelling detectives, solving murders, finding ghosts, hunting the deer, poaching, fishing the rivers, and running with the hounds. Such wonderful dreams. Just being here brought back the first tears since given the news of Jane and his parents.

Jane was an orphan of a friend of his Father, who, along with his wife had been killed whilst skiing on Helvellyn, the highest mountain in the Lakes. Simon and his wife had brought her up as a Daughter and it was the happiest moment of their lives when Mark told them that they were to be married.

'How are you then, Mara?'

'Oh! fine,' answered the old man. 'A bit of arthritis now and then but we still manage to walk the fells and do the hound trailing. Bracken's just the same as always, the best dog in the county.'

'What about Niall?'

'By George, Mark,' striking his forehead with the palm of his hand, 'l should have told you straight away. He's back, came back a year ago. Been working in Ireland, staying at my sisters, of all places. He'll be over the moon to see you.'

Mark thought to himself, 'Poor Mara, no one ever told him of the fight over Jane.' He wondered what would be said when they met.

'How long are you going to be here, son?'

'Well,' said Mark, 'I've got to look over the place, sort out the affairs and arranged the funeral.'

'Funeral's already been arranged, son. Sir Arthur, from Ravenglass, has done all that. He heard you would be home soon, and after all he was your dad and mam's best friend. His daughter Stella has been here nearly every day to collect messages and tidy the house for you. Niall and myself and a couple of the estate farmers have cleared up the bomb damage, so the house is livable. Stella has made a temporary kitchen until things are sorted out with you. Come on, I'll make you a cup of tea and then I'll walk up to the house with you; perhaps a whiskey might help mull the time away.'

After about an hour of talking about old times, Mark said, 'Look Mara, if its OK with you, I would like to go up there by myself, just to be alone for a while.'

'Sure son,' said Mara, 'I understand. Are you going to stay at the house while you're home?'

'Not tonight,' replied Mark, 'I'm booked in at the Kings Head, but I'll be around for a week or two. I have to report back to Naval Headquarters to let them know what I'm doing as well. I'm lucky they've given me some time off, with the war and all that. See you later old friend. Oh! Don't tell Niall I'm home yet, I'm sure we'll get together soon.' With a wave of his hand he left the caravan.

'Here Bracken,' Mara shouted, as the dog tried to follow Mark up the track.

CHAPTER TEN

Aunt Margaret was waiting at the front door of the farmhouse as the pony and trap pulled to a halt. David jumped off first and ran to his aunt, giving her a hug. Pulling him to her ample bosom she swung him round in a circle. 'Oh! Welcome, the both of you, it's so good to have you here. I've got a hot pot on the stove all ready for us, we'll have lots of fun.' Then, calling to her husband, 'Ray, take their luggage upstairs.'

Out from the house bounded a large dog.

'Bramble, it's you, really you?'

Recognising the children immediately, the dog began to chase its own tail in its excitement.

'Give over, Bram,' shouted Ray, 'get in the house all of you, I'm starving.'

Picking up the baggage, Ray went in ahead of them whilst Margaret, holding both Heather and David to her side, followed behind. They entered the lounge where the floor was made from the thick slate from the hillside quarries. In the centre of the room a large table was set out ready for their dinner, a silver candelabra standing in the middle. Bramble curled up on a rug in front of the open fireplace, which, though not yet alight, had been cleaned and ready, for although the days in May were warm, the nights on the hillside were still quite cold and damp.

Removing their coats, the children followed their aunt into the kitchen where, on a large iron stove, simmered a giant hotpot, steam rising through the half-inch thick pastry crust. From the oven came the aroma of baking bread. Aunt Margaret was renowned through the valley for her baking, and for many years had won first prize at the Egremont fair near Whitehaven, an annual event for country folk. In June she was going to enter the Ambleside fair which was even larger and more prestigious.

Ray came down the stairs carrying two plates, a candle placed on each. 'There you are, I'll leave them on the sideboard for you for this evening. After dinner I'll be going onto the fells for an hour, we lost two chickens this morning and I've noticed that the corner of the potato patch has been dug up. Either we've got some Seathwaite kids playing about, or the foxes are having chicken and chips tonight. 'Come on woman,' he shouted to Margaret, 'the children must be hungry by now.'

CHAPTER ELEVEN

Richter and Stelmach sat in the body of the plane's fuselage, gnawing away at a chicken carcass and taking bites of baked potatoes that they had cooked over a small fire. This was washed down by a cup of coffee that they had in their survival kits. Earlier that morning they had managed to cross a river by climbing up the side of a waterfall to the highest point, then jumping from stone to stone to the other side.

About a mile down the valley from where they were resting stood a farm with a stone road leading through a small copse. They could see the road heading northwards over another hill then disappearing from view. Southwards, the road climbed up a mountainside. They looked back across the river from where they had come from. To their left, the woodland stretched out of sight, whilst to their right, it climbed up for about a quarter of a mile into the hill side, above which the mountain was covered with shale and slate, crushed by millions of years of ice and snow. At the summit of the mountain, a ledge of rock over-hung some two hundred feet. To the right of the mountain, they could see the ancient sheep tracks, still used by the sheep that they could observe in the distance.

'Its beautiful isn't it?' remarked Horst. 'Look at those colours, I wish I had my paintbrush with me.'

'Survival is our aim at the moment little friend, but if the weather stays warm and if we have food and cover, we should be ok until then we find Major Bauer. We will try and get near that farm and see what we can find, but go carefully – they've probably got dogs.'

CHAPTER TWELVE

Niall O'Leary was staggered when a new police-sergeant had walked into the shop and gave the password, his heart was thumping so hard that he thought it would burst apart.

The day he left home, following the fight with Mark, he had walked across the hills to Whitehaven some thirty miles away, boarded a ship to Ireland, and worked his way down to Wexford in the South, hitching a ride from Belfast. He knew his Grandparents lived there somewhere, though he had never met them. His mother's parents had died before he was born and he didn't even know his mother's maiden name. Fortunately he had sold his car to Oliver Clark, the ironmonger, and so had enough money to last him for a few months. Arriving in the town, he checked in at a bed and breakfast. That evening, in a local bar named 'Flanagans', he asked the Landlord if there were any O'Leary's in the town. Three men, who had been sitting quietly across the room, murmured to each other. The one who had been sitting nearest to him stood up and approached the bar. Turning to look at Niall, he asked, 'What would the likes of you be wanting with the O'Leary?'

Niall, stretching his six-foot frame, answered, 'If it's any of your business, they happen to be my grandparents that I'm looking for.'

'To be sure, the O'Leary's have only there own kin hear, and I don't recall ever seeing you before.'

Niall, now getting somewhat heated, replied, 'Look, if you know an O'Leary, either tell me or butt out.'

'His two friends got up in the corner, but the one at the bar waved them back down. 'Now that's no way to behave, but you have no Irish brogue with you, you sound more English than any part of Ireland I know.'

'That's because I was born in Lancashire, therefore I suppose I'm a Lancastrian. But being English doesn't mean a jot to me. I've never met my Grandparents and they probably have never heard of me. But if you know something, then my father's name was Martin, nicknamed Mara when be came to Lancashire.'

'Well then, and what is your name?'

'Niall, I believe that was my Great-grandfathers name. My Grandfather is Sean and my Grandmother Mary.

'Does anybody know those names?' shouted the man at the bar to the others.

They shook their heads. 'Sorry, no.'

'Never mind, we'll keep an eye and an ear open for you.'

The barman shook his head as the three left the bar. Carefully putting down the glass that he had been polishing all through the discussion said, 'look boy, steer well clear of those three. They are trouble, with three capital letters, if you no what I mean.'

About an hour later the bar had filled up with more than a couple of dozen people, when, through the door, came the Irishman who had confronted him at the bar. Behind him came an older man, well into his seventies. He was wearing a sheepskin coat and a trilby that had obviously seen a lot of rain. Niall looked at him warily. He noticed that his hands were large yet his fingers were very small. 'I bet he's got a hell of a grip,' thought Niall, as the stranger was pulled a pint of Guinness. As he had never opened his mouth it was easy to assume that he was well known to the barman. As the old man approached a table next to Niall, the occupants stood up and moved away. The stranger, swivelling his chair around so that he had his back to Niall, turned his head.

'Your Mothers Name?' He said nothing else, just stareing into Niall's eyes.

'Your Mothers name?'

'Er! Mary. Why?' stammered Niall.

'Your Fathers name?'

'Martin. Look, what's it got to do with you?'

'Is your mother and father alive?'

'My dad is, my mother died when I was about two.'

'What did she die of?'

'That's now't to do with you,' shouted Niall, and began to get up.

'Sit down. Now.'

Niall was now becoming agitated by the steel blue look in the old mans eyes, reminding him of his own father's way of commanding attention.

'What did your mother die of?' repeated the old man.

'Poisoned Mushrooms.'

The old man took a sip of his drink and quietly said, 'and was she the only one?'

'No. I lost four sisters.'

The old man nodded. 'Son, I am Sean O'Leary, your Grandfather. Get your gear, your coming home.'

CHAPTER THIRTEEN

Bauer descended the stairs of the Manor Inn, still weary after taking four hours sleep. It was almost twenty-four hours since he had left the airfield in France, and until he hit the pillow, had no idea of how tired he had been. He had washed, shaved and changed out of the uniform into a sweater and a pair of clean trousers that the 'late' Peter Thompson had unknowingly bequeathed him. As murder was not part of his make up, he had reflected over the death of the policeman; but it had been the business of self-survival. He hoped his colleagues had made it back to home base, but this was not the time or place to dwell on it. He'd been extremely lucky up to now, but his time would be short out here in the middle of nowhere. He had to sit down at sometime with O'Leary and formulate a plan.

His main objective had been to gather information about the coastal business between Barrow and Workington, what were Vickers building, and what were the steel works at Barrow, Millom and Whitehaven manufacturing? As 'Thompson,' he also had a brief to look for a spy. This wasn't a problem, he already knew who he was. But he was intrigued by what was going on at Ravenglass Castle. Why should an English Police Superintendent want to join him in meeting a British industrialist. No doubt he would find out in a couple of days time.

As he entered the hotel lounge, he was amused by the sight of some thirty or more men trying to get to the bar, all dressed alike in black suits, white ties and shirts. As he came through the door, there was a lull in the talking, which, after a cautious glance, one of the men came up to him.

'You will be Sergeant Thompson then, are you?'

'Yes sir,' he replied.

'Let me introduce myself, I am Arthur Duckworth, and for my sins, Master of Ulpha Lodge No. 125. We are about to have our social in the dining room so I haven't much time to make introductions to some of our Brethren. But you know Oliver Clark I believe.'

Bauer nodded at Clark, 'Good evening sir.'

'Oh! No sirs here please, call me Oliver. Come on Sir Arthur, we had better be getting upstairs. Brethren,' he shouted, 'dining now, no more smoking please.'

Sir Arthur patted Bauer on the back. 'Sorry Sergeant, but I believe we will be meeting on Friday.'

Before Bauer could ask the reason why, Sir Arthur turned and left. Within a few minutes the room was entirely empty. Bauer went up to the bar and ordered a whisky. From the taproom that ran adjacent to the bar he could hear the noise of men talking.

'Jacks out!' a voice shouted.

Intrigued, he made his way into the other bar, where a group of men stood around an oblong mahogany table. 'You want one Fred?' demanded one of the men sat at the table.

'Aye, lad,' came the reply.

'You George?'

'Yes please,' another acknowledged.

The German observed that it was Niall O'leary dealing out the cards, tossing them one by one to each of the men in turn, then placing a card on the table as he called each by name.

'That's it then?'

The dealer kept on going around the table placing a card on top of the others. When as a Jack came up he called, 'you're first out Sid, you next Alf, Dennis, George.' As the fourth jack was laid he stopped. 'Your choice, Sid.'

'Crib it will be then.' an old man called back through the clouds of his smoking pipe.

The four at the table stood up and let those that had received 'Jacks' sit down. Niall nodded to Bauer and went over to the far corner alcove and sat down. Bauer, noticing what O'Leary was drinking, went to the bar and ordered a Guinness and a whiskey. The noise had quietened down except for the whispered 'Fifteen two and two for a pair,' as each card player called out their scores. Occasionally a laugh came from the watchers as a player made an error. 'You plonker, that should be a Queen laid.' The banter continued.

Bauer went over to O'Leary, 'Good evening, nice to see you again.'

'How the hell have you got here in that uniform, and where did you come in from?' whispered Niall, glancing around.

'Time for questions later,' said Bauer, 'but for now I want to know what your movements are for tomorrow.'

'I'm off to the timber yard in Barrow, to get some wood for Mr., Clark. I go every Wednesday and Saturday morning. I have lunch at the 'Crows Nest Hotel,' - that's where I pick up my information - from the lads who work in Vickers and some of the sailors off the submarines,' explained Niall.

'They come in for an afternoon break from sea trials,' he went on to explain, 'I belong to the dominoes team and its surprising what I pick up.'

'Where do you transmit your information from?'

'I have my radio transmitter set up in an abandoned copper mine on Walna Scar.'

'Right then O'Leary.'

'Hang on, what do I call you?' asked Niall.

'Peter' replied Bauer, 'when I am not on duty, Sergeant Thompson when I am. What's your name then?'

'My mates call me Peddlar, after living in a caravan nearly all my life.'

'Where's your Caravan?'

'Between Ulpha and Seathwaite, on Simom Hughlock's estate. Go canny round there, one of your lot dropped a bomb on the big house, a friend of mine was killed,'

Bauer looked carefully at Peddler. 'Altered your feelings about us at all?' he said with an edge of menace in his voice.

'I'm not to happy, but I suppose war is war,' Niall replied.

The German felt a tinge of unease, and thought he would keep a careful eye on him for now. Finished in getting the information he required for now, Bauer emptied his glass and got up. 'I'm just going over to the police station, but tonight I want you to transmit a message saying all is well. The message is in this cigarette packet, decode it and transmit at midnight. From now on, pass all your information to me and close your transmitter down until further notice, understand?'

Peddlar nodded, placed his empty glass on the table, and left.

Horst Bauer waited a moment and then went out and crossed the road into the police Station.

P.C. Basset, the younger of the two constables, called out 'Evening Sarge. Settled in?'

'Yes thank you,' he replied, 'how are you doing?'

'Very quiet, no excitement tonight. You should have been here the other night; all hell let loose when those German bastards killed Simon, Leslie and Mark Hughloch's wife. Scum like that should be stood against the wall and shot. I wish I could get hold of them. The funeral is on Friday morning at eleven. Inspector Moses will be here before going to Ravenglass with Sir Duckworth. There should be a fair crowd of mourners at Seathwaite Church.. Do you reckon we will need support from other parish coppers?'

'I'll let you know tomorrow,' said Bauer, 'I will be having a look around the area myself.'

Basset escorted him around the rest of the building. Observing only one policeman on duty, Bauer asked, 'Where's your other officer?'

'Oh! He finished his shift at eight, he's back in the morning at eight.'

'Very well then, good night, you know where to find me if needed.'

Leaving the building he walked down the square, past the joiner's shop, and crossed over the road, entering the King's Head, a three hundred years old timber-framed building. Inside, the walls were hung with plates, pots, brasses, and, over the fireplace, a painting of a seventeenth century coach. Even on warm summers evenings the glowing embers within the fireplace gave a traditional English sign of hospitality to all that entered.

'You must be the new Sergeant?' called a voice from behind the bar. The landlord was a small but portly man with a large whiskered moustache and beard. He was wearing a leather smock or waistcoat that seemed too small for his frame, and in his mouth a clay pipe protruded. Altogether he gave the appearance of someone who had just stepped out of his own picture.

'First drink on the house, Sergeant,' he said, 'and the next on him,' laughingly pointing to the young man who was standing by the bar. 'I'm George Purcell, licensee of the King's Head and this,' pointing his finger, 'is Mark Hughlock.'

'Glad to have you with us, Sergeant, though I must admit you could not come to a quieter place. Only poachers and picnickers to deal with,' smiled Mark, offering his hand.

'Pleased to meet you to Mr. Hemlock,' said Bauer.

'Hughlock, Officer. Please call me Mark, every one else does. I will probably get to talk to you later on but I'm afraid I can't stop.' He turned and waved his hand. 'Good night all.' Mark went through the rear of the pub and up to his room.

'Lives here does he?' Bauer nodded in the direction of the departing officer.

'No, only a temporary measure; he is here to bury his wife and parents killed in the bombing the other day. He's a Commander in the Royal Navy now, done very well for himself, poor chap. Funerals at the end of the week.'

'Yes I know. I didn't know that was the son though. Tragic isn't it?'

CHAPTER FOURTEEN

Mark stood at the entrance to his home. It was an early Georgian building, built on the site of an earlier building that had been destroyed by the Scots in 1744, a time when his Great-Great-Grandfather was a famous army surgeon under the Duke of Cumberland. On entering the massive double oak door, he was surprised to find it unlocked. Crossing the threshold and into the Great-hall, where suits-of-armour, shields, and crossed swords were intermingled with a gallery of his parent's ancestors, he was met by the winding mahogany staircase, at the head of which stood a stuffed bear, standing in a rampant position, as if guarding the house from intruders. As his father always said, 'It's my Tyler.' Being the founder of the Masonic Lodge in Broughton, he had the Lodge named after the house.

All seemed so strangely the same as he passed through the hall into the library. Except for that faint yet pungent smell of burnt wood, there was no sign of any damage; all the plates, paintings and many vases still in place. At the far end of the library he opened another door which took him into the dining room. In front of him stood the oak dining table, around which twenty-four people could be seated. 'No apparent sign of damage here either,' he thought to himself, though the smell was getting stronger. Again he carried on to another door at the end of the room and opened it. Broken chairs and a table were leaning against the wall of what was a corridor to the kitchen, but with one side of the corridor demolished, he was immediately able to gain sight of what had been the kitchen.

Everything was black and charred, the moonlight eerily illuminated what had been the far wall of the combined kitchen and conservatory. He stepped over the remains and looked around, tears welling up in his eyes, when he suddenly heard a noise behind him. Spinning round, he was met by the sight of a beautiful dark haired woman.

He gasped. 'Jane!' Then, pulling himself together, 'Oh! Sorry, who are you?'

The young woman, about five feet seven in height, slim, with dark yet sultry eyes, smiled at him. 'I guess you must be Mark Hughlock. I'm sorry I startled you, but I was just checking the premises. Oh! I'm sorry, let me introduce myself. I'm Stella Duckworth, Sir Arthur's daughter.'

They shook hands politely.

'Lets get out of here,' he shuddered. Then, realising that he had not eaten all day, turned to her and enquired, 'I don't think I can face looking around here much longer, do you fancy a drink and a bite to eat? You could tell me all about yourself and bring me up to date with all that's going on. There's a small pub called 'High Cross' on the outskirts of Broughton. That is, unless you have you eaten?'

'Thank you Mark, I would love that.' As she walked passed him he smelt the scent of her perfume. He shook his head sadly as he followed her out.

Mara O'Leary was standing by his car. He smiled, 'Ok Master Mark, you have met then?' Niall's called,but I haven't told him your home yet. I don't understand why you won't let me tell him.'

'Ok, Mara, I'll be probably see him tomorrow. Goodnight and thanks for everything,' affectionately patting him on the back.

CHAPTER FIFTEEN

It was early morning, and Heather and Margaret were inside the barn feeding the chickens. Tess and Max, the sheep dogs, were tethered by a chain to a large kennel. Unlike Bramble, they were kept outside. Heather went over to Mabel, the pony, and, after first giving her a carrot, placed a nose bag on her. The air was fresh and clean, and through the open doors came the aroma of baled hay being warmed by the early morning sun. Heather gazed at the fells and mountainside, the mist hanging like a canopy of candyfloss that her parents bought her when she was on holiday at Blackpool. Suddenly, as if by one of God's miracles of nature, the mist was surrounded by a rainbow which passed directly over the valley. As she stood by the door, the sun outlined her lithe but graceful body, showing the roundness of her breasts so firm, so young, the contours of her legs and narrowness of her hips showing youth and beauty which made Margaret instinctively feel her own. Heather looked around. Immediately Margaret dropped her hand to her sides, embarrassed by her own thoughts of yesteryears when she was a pretty young girl herself.

'We'd better go and make the beds then. Your Uncle Ray will be checking the sheep on the fells soon, and will want his breakfast when he gets back. Would you like to take David to Seathwaite School in the pony and trap later on?'

Oh! Yes please, Aunt,' excited at the thought of being in charge.

'Right then,' her Aunt replied, 'I will get Ray to couple Mabel up before he leaves.'

They went into the kitchen. Ray was just finishing his tea. He agreed to bridle and couple the horse's rig, and half an hour later they set off for the hills, the two collies running ahead. They were about half way up the fell when he they met Niall O'Leary coming down.

'Good morning, Peddlar,' said Ray, 'how is your Dad? Not seen him for a while.'

'Oh! He's ok, busy getting the pheasant eggs turned. They will be hatching in a couple of weeks. I don't know if the shoot will be on this year or what, with Simon Hughlock gone.'

'Oh! Well,' shouted Ray, 'you can ask Master Mark when you see him; he's at the King's Head.'

'Mark's home?' exclaimed Peddler.

'Why yes, came in yesterday with our nephew and niece. Morning then.'

'Morning,' replied Peddler.

'It's six years, almost to the day, since Mark and I quarreled,' he reminisced. He decided that, if they met, he would not tell him that it was he who had found Jane and his family. 'How have I got myself into this mess? He thought to himself. All had been so clear to him, but now, seeing poor Jane lying there, and what was left of Mark's Mother and Father who had, for nearly eighteen years, treated him as Mark's brother, what he was now doing seemed so futile. He wished his Grandfather were around to give the same support that he had in Ireland. He reflected on those years away from home.

CHAPTER SIXTEEN

Wexford, in the south-east of Ireland, is, compared with Waterford and Cork, a small fishing village, yet an insecurity seemed difficult to explain when he met all who spoke to him. Except his Grandfather that is. He was a giant of a man, though his Grandmother was completely opposite, only five feet tall, grey-haired and her eyes dark brown. She talked incessantly, even when Sean was talking, chattering as if what ever she was going to say she would start and finish when she was good and ready.

'Oh! My darling lad. Oh! It's lovely to see you. Oh! You were only two when we last saw you. Oh! You just look just like your mother. Oh! ….'

Shut up, woman,' chided Sean. 'Let he boy get through the door. Niall,' he called, 'let me introduce you to your Uncle David, Uncle Jacob, and Uncle Carriag, your father's brothers.

Peddlar gasped, 'I'm sorry,' he said, excusing himself, 'believe me, I didn't know Dad had any brothers.'

'He's no brother of mine and you better believe it.' snarled Carriag.

'Whished! now,' said his grandmother, 'that's all in the past and don't you forget it; there will be no more bitterness here.'

There was a knock on the door and Carriag's hand went under his jacket.

'Don't you dare,' Sean glared, 'keep that out of sight.'

His wife went to the door, and three men of similar age to Peddlar came into the lounge. Grandmother had just shut the door when there was another knock. Mary again opened it and a young woman entered, her deep blue eyes, and ample figure standing proud from a green sweater, her lips were red, and even in the candle lit room he could see that she had no need for make up. Peddlar reckoned that she was about a year or so younger than himself.

'Come in Mary. Niall, this is Mary Ryan, David's girlfriend. He's out with your other cousins, Cohn and Brendan.' She hesitated, giving a startled glance at Sean.

'On business. They will be back tomorrow.'

'Now that the introductions are over, I'll make us all some supper. Come on Mary, give me a hand in the kitchen,' she called.

'Hang on mother, Carriag called after them, 'we can't stop. We've business ourselves tonight.'

Sean gave a muted ok. 'You know what you are about, watch yourself,' pointing a warning finger at Carriag. 'Don't do anything stupid.'

Mary Ryan came back into the lounge and Sean said softly, 'Mary, sweetheart, nip over the road and get Niall's baggage from the pub; he'll be our guest for as long as he wants.'

Niall protested, 'Oh! I don't want to put you to any trouble.'

'Trouble son,' said Sean 'is our middle name.'

'Now Sean, your not to involve Niall in any of your shenanigans.' Sean's wife shook her fist in determination, then, turning to her Grandson, 'Now Niall, tell me about your life in England.'

'Lancashire, Grandma, Lancashire,' corrected Niall, 'England has no call on me.'

For about an hour he talked about the fells, the eagles, the occasional deer, the breeding of the pheasant. But every time he started to talk about his father, the subject was changed, much to the chagrin of his Grandmother. Finally he stifled a yawn, and that seemed, to all, the time to retire to their beds.

Young Mary said, 'well I better be off then.'

'May I walk you home,' offered Niall.

'No thank you, I only live across the road but I will see you tomorrow.' Then, after blowing a kiss to the old couple, she left.

Sean yawned, 'Come on son, I'll show you your room. Down in a minute Ma.' Having safely seen Peddler to his room Sean came down, his wife whispered, 'Please Sean, don't involve the boy.'

'I'm sorry Ma, but he could be useful to the cause, and he is of our blood. We will not discuss this until all the lads are back tomorrow.'

Lighting a candle he put his arm around her waist. 'Come on Ma. Bed.'

CHAPTER SEVENTEEN

Heather, having returned from taking David to school, which was only about two miles or so down the valley, led Mabel into the barn.

'Everything ok dear?' queried her aunt.

'Yes aunt, he met some of his friends from last year so he is quite happy. Is there anything you wish me to do?'

'No dear, come and have your breakfast. Ray is a bit late so I'll put his in the oven.'

For a while they talked small talk about how her mother and father were doing at Uncle Jim's and Aunt Nancy's, and what it was like during the blackout. Questioned inquisitively, Heather told her aunt about the air-raid sirens and how they had to huddle in the Anderson shelters in the back garden. She told her about her fear when the bomb dropped at Ulpha, and how she had met Mark Hughlock on the train.

Then they heard the dogs barking and the chattering stopped. Bramble got up from the rug by the fire and went to the door. There was a stamping on the ground outside as Ray cleared the mud from his boots before entering.

'I've lost a sheep,' he growled. 'Damn queer. If it were a fox or an eagle, there would be some sign or a bit of carcass, but nothing. Damn queer,' he repeated. 'I think I'll pop into Broughton this afternoon and see the Bobbie.'

'See the pub more like,' Margaret scolded.

Heather, looking at the fells through the window, enquired, 'Aunt Margaret, do you mind if I go for a walk?'

'All right dear, but be back before three o'clock to pick David up from school, and,' she paused, 'I want to get some shopping from the village.'

Grabbing her cardigan from the back of a chair, Heather quickly walked out of the farm door, Bramble following behind. 'Is it all right for me to take Bramble?' she shouted back into the house.

'Yes dear.' replied her aunt.

Heather crossed the field to the five-barred gate, keeping a wary eye on the cows lying on the grass. 'Come on Bramble.' She shouted. They followed the track until they reached the fells. Here and there she could see patches of bilberry growing in clusters and the meadows of heather, after which her mother had named her, were coloured a bright purple. The sun was now due south and high in the sky. With perspiration forming between her breasts, she removed her cardigan, tying the sleeves around her waist. Bramble suddenly stopped and stared intently at a patch of ferns. Then, with a sudden surge and flurry, a brace of grouse took off with a screech, and flew along the valley.

'Come on Bramble, leave them be.'

Humming happily to herself, Heather continued on up the fell side, turned right along a sheep track, and then crossed over a dry stone wall until she reached the start of the forest. Bramble chased a pheasant which 'cockled' angrily at being disturbed, whilst rabbits bolted back into the wood, in fright at the dog's sudden appearance. After walking along the edge of the woods for about half a mile, she came to the river.

Bramble jumped in and splashed his way across, whilst Heather crossed by the stepping stones. The river meandered around the hillside to the waterfalls, but Heather decided to take a short cut over the hill through the tall bracken. By the time she the summit, she was feeling totally exhausted and sat down, admiring the view. Picking a long blade of grass, she put it between her teeth and lay back, loosening her cardigan from her waist. As the sun's heat beat down she undid the buttons of her dress, unclasped her bra, and placed it by her side. Then, opening her frock, she let the sun warm her as she listened to the babbling of the water as it tumbled over the rocks.

She had only been lying there for a moment or two when Bramble gave a low growl. At first couldn't see anything, but then, as she was about to stand up, she noticed a young man emerging from the woods on the far side of the river. Pressing herself into the soft grass to avoid being seen, she whispered to Bramble, 'Stay.' Carefully moving the sheltering bracken to one side, her naked breasts leaning on the damp grass under her, she noticed that, as the young man walked along the riverbank, he appeared to be looking around somewhat furtively. 'He must be about nineteen or twenty,' she thought, observing his short blonde hair, greyish uniform, and knee length boots.

Heather gasped as he sat down and took his boots and jacket off, as she could not help but feel the nipples on her breasts begin to rise and she felt a tightness in her throat. The man looked around again and, as he began to take his trousers off, she suppressed a silly giggle with her hand. By now he was now down to his shorts and socks. She noticed that his chest was hairless; like her father's. 'He is very attractive,' she thought.

Holding onto the trunk of a tree for support, the man was now removing his shorts. Heather was in rapture; his bottom was tight and firm. He turned towards her, and for a moment she froze, she couldn't help but look between his legs. She had seen her brother's tassle many times, but from what she could remember, it was never as big as that. At school the other girls would brag about the size of their boy friend's 'prick'. Heather sniggered quietly to herself.

The man scrambled over the stones and put a hand into the waterfall, as if testing the temperature. Holding his breath as he stood under the cascading water, then ran his fingers through his hair and over his body. Feeling every movement with him, Heather began fondling her breasts, and as his hands went down to his thighs so did hers. For a moment he held the thing between his legs, and almost involuntary she placed her own hands into her knickers, twisting the hairs that only recently had begun to grow there. She was beginning to feel strange things that she had never felt before. She turned on he back and began to play with herself.

Bramble growled, as if bringing her to her senses. She looked up again, the stranger had left the waterfall and was now lying on his back, the sun drying his naked body. She watched him as be grasped his tassel, and as he stroked it up and down, she could see it rising and rising. He began slowly and then his pace began to quicken until he ejaculated. Heather felt she could hardly breath as the man then stood up and walked back into the river to wash himself. Bramble started to growl again. As she turned to quieten him she noticed that the man was looking up into the woods where, about twenty five yards away, another stranger stood leaning against a fir tree, smoking a cigarette. He smiled to himself and was about to turn when he thought he saw something flash on the hill side.

He stared intently, but then shrugged his shoulders and walked back into the trees.

Hans Stellmach finished dressing and followed his companion into the cover of the forest. Heather, edged back through the bracken and replaced her bra. She felt so elated that she never even gave thought to finding out who the men were. She just felt for the first time in her life that she had become a woman. Finally dressed, she called to Bramble and ran down the valley towards the farm, vowing to return the following day to see if that man was still around.

CHAPTER EIGHTEEN

Bauer, or, in his new pseudonym, 'Thompson,' called at he police station early the next morning. 'Any messages?' he inquired.

'Yes, Sarge, phone call from Ray Morgan. Would like to see you this afternoon, thinks he may have sheep rustlers.'

'Fine. Was there anything else?'

'Yes, Niall O'Leary would like to see you at the shop. He says that there's been prowlers around his dad's caravan. He's not afraid of prowlers; its what his dad, Mara, would do to them that bothers him.'

'Mara. That's a strange name?'

'It's the Cumberland and Westmoreland name for a miners mate,' explained the constable, 'Old Mara has been living in that caravan on the Hughlock estate before I was born.'

Right then constable, I'll go and see this O'Leary. What have you two got lined up?'

P.C. Basset laughed. 'Black out reports. Lights showing at some of the shops, and at a couple of farms. We'll have to chase them up and warn them that even in a village, the fines are just the same.'

P.C. Bill Wordsworth looked at his report book. 'I'm off to the Church at Seathwaite, to organise traffic control for the funeral tomorrow.'

'Fine, see you later today then,' willing them to get on with their business. The German decided to leave his bike where it was and walked down to the joiner's shop, Thompson was looking through the front window when 'Peddlar' turned around. Acknowledging his presence, Niall nodded toward the side alley of the shop. A few moments later he came out carrying some copper pipes. 'I am off down to Barrow to exchange these pipes and collect some timber; is there anything you want me to look out for?'

'No more than you already do. Find out what damage was done in the last raid, and pick up any gossip. Meet me tonight at six o'clock, I will be transmitting from my room at eight o'clock and I want you to keep an eye open so that I am not disturbed.'

The Sergeant then walked back to the main road and Niall climbed into a pick-up truck, reversing out of the alley and into the street. Thompson gave a mock salute as he waved him on his way. He was about to walk off into the town when two Austin-Seven saloon cars followed by a Bentley came round the corner and parked in front of the Police station. As he walked cautiously back up the road, the rear door of the Bentley opened and out stepped a Police Officer. As he drew near, the Police Superintendent caught sight of him.

'Good timing. You of course must be Thompson?'

Bauer stood to attention and saluted. 'Yes sir, good morning.'

The senior officer introduced himself. 'Superintendent Moses, please come on in and we'll talk.' As they entered the station, Basset and Wordsworth jumped to attention, straightened their ties, and saluted.

'Two teas, constable,' smiled Thompson, 'and three outside for the drivers. My office sir?'

They entered the office and the Superintendent sat down. Thompson remained standing.

'Sit down Sergeant,' pointing at the vacant chair, 'I will be returning tomorrow to elaborate more on what is going on in the area. I must caution you that this is highly confidential, but having obtained the use of these two cars last evening,' indicating to the two vehicles outside the window, 'I decided that speed was of the essence.' These two cars have been specially fitted with antennas to receive and locate illegal transmissions to the enemy. Police stations throughout the country are utilising specially trained operatives to teach their own officers how to operate them. You, having come straight from London, have this experience, right?'

Thompson smiled and nodded. If only the inspector knew that he probably had more experience in radio transmissions than the whole UK police force.

'Right Thompson, first take your two constables out today. Make a dummy transmission with the two drivers and I will transmit a signal from some where on the moors. I have got the rest of this morning, and up to two thirty this afternoon, for you to get it right, ok?'

'Yes sir,' replied Thompson dutifully.

'Right, when we've completed these trials I will take the other drivers back to Millom. Now then, as you were told in your briefing in London, there appears to be an agent operating somewhere in the hills or villages of this district. One of your transmitters can be set up in this evening here in the station, whilst you and a constable can patrol the area. The transmissions have always been on the hour, but never every hour, so a constant twenty-four hour watch has to be kept, especially over the next four days.'

'Why four days sir?' enquired Thompson.

'I will tell you that tomorrow after the funeral of Simon Hughlock's family. For security reasons we shall be meeting at the Hughlock residence instead of Ravenglass Castle. No word of this, even to your staff, all right?'

'Yes sir.'

There was a knock at the door and Wordsworth entered, carrying a tray of tea and biscuits.

'Fine then Sergeant, we shall have this and be on our way.'

CHAPTER NINETEEN

Mark Hughloch had enjoyed his meal with Stella. She was a very exuberant young woman, the only daughter of Sir Arthur and Sylvia Duckworth. Sir Arthur had made his fortune in the electrical services industry and was a great contributor to Masonic and non-Masonic charities, being a co-founder, together with Mark's father, of the Ulpha Lodge. Mark had known Stella for a short time at an infant school in Gosforth, but then she had gone off to a private school, Holmrook in Cumberland, shortly after her father had been knighted. This was their first meeting in nearly fourteen years. He looked at her over the dining table and thought she was indeed a radiant and lovely woman, not greatly unlike Jane, and again a strain of the tragedy came over him.

'It must be a very difficult time for you Mark,' Stella said sympathetically, noticing the furrow appearing on his forehead.

He looked at her and smiled. 'You would think that with the destruction and death I have seen in the past eighteen months, I would have coped better.'

'Mark,' she said softly, 'there is no league table on grief you know. Everyone feels as you do. They had many friends, and on Friday you will notice that. Everything is arranged that can be arranged. Father has offered our home for the reception of their close friends. I will go over the list tomorrow evening with you, so you have nothing to concern your self with. Did Jane have no other family but you and your parents?'

'Put Mara and Niall O'Leary on that list,' he said, as if diverting the subject, 'they may not come, but I will try to invite them myself. Niall was,' he hesitated, 'very fond of Jane.'

'All right, Mark' she smiled, comfortingly. 'Well I'm afraid I must leave now, can we meet here again tomorrow?'

'Fine, Stella. Give me your phone number in case of problems. My love and thanks to your mother and father.' As Stella began to offer him a lift down into Broughton, Mark interupted. 'No need to worry, it's only fifteen minutes walk and the night air will freshen me up, its been a long day.'

The couple shook hands, Stella got into her car and drove off towards Duddon, using the short cut over Corney Fell, Mark walked slowly back to the village and entered the pub. He was gazing into his second pint of 'Cases Bitter' when the Landlord introduced him to the new policeman.

CHAPTER TWENTY

Mara O'Leary, sat by the camp fire alongside his caravan, the last drop of the 'Bells' whiskey was still in his glass. He lay back in his rocking chair and looked up at he sky, Bramble at his feet. Silhouetted by the line of the crags of Scarfell pike, and to the left the tumbling fell side, rose, above Walna Scar, the peak of Coniston Old Man. Even though it was coming to the end of May, there were still drifts of snow in the crevices two thousand feet above sea level.

He loved to sit here like this, the stars twinkling, the smell of fresh clean air, the gentle but constant fall of water over the rocks in the Duddon river. His favourite constellation was the 'Plough' or 'Northern Cross.' He thought of his wife and his children who had died so horribly many years ago, and how he had named each star after them so that he could personally talk to them at night. Oh! Yes, he often went down to Seathwaite Churchyard to their grave, but here he was alone and at one with them. He raised his glass to the heavens and saluted, 'To you, my loves!'

He poured himself another 'two fingers' and gave thought to Niall. Five years had gone by since Niall's return. He had long ago guessed why he had suddenly left, but could not see why Niall had not confided in him. He had seen it coming, but just thought it was a crush since it seemed obvious to all that Jane doted on Mark, looking upon Niall simply as a brother. 'Still, love is blind. God knows I have suffered enough because of that Bloody 1916.

Mara was nineteen years of age at the time of the Dublin uprising. His father was quartermaster in the Wexford IRA. From the age of ten, their father had inducted him and his brothers into the squad. 'Freedom for all Ireland' to rid the British by any means; that's what hurt Martin. 'By any means.' There was a thrill in attacking guard-posts and docks, and stealthily attacking sentries, but the cold blooded bombings which indiscriminately killed their own people as well, sickened him. And then there was 'Shelagh.' Kevin Ryan and his wife Shelagh were part of Martin's command. She was a tough, ruthless girl, and had married Kevin only a few months before, on the rebound from Martin, with whom she had been going out together for about a year. When Martin caught her and Kevin in bed after coming home slightly injured after escaping a British patrol, Shelagh had begged his forgiveness. But Martin was adamant, 'leave me alone and take him with you or I'll kill the little bastard.'

On January 1st 1917 a raid was planned on the docks at Rosslare Harbour, where a large shipment of explosives had just been unloaded. Martin's group were to attack the guard-post. David and Jacob's own two squads were to place explosives at the gas works; Carriag, along with Kevin, were to blow up the ammunition depot. Martin was against the idea from the start and almost came to blows with Carriag.

'Don't be a yellow bastard,' Carriag had snarled during the meeting the night before. 'If you haven't got the guts, I'll do it myself.'

Martin started to rise from his chair, his fists clenched in anger, when his Father said, 'Enough! Any fighting here will be against the British.'

Martin argued profusely. 'But its not against the bloody British, its against the whole town. If that arms depot and gasworks blow, innocent people are going to get hurt.

'No,' contradicted his father, 'the docks are far enough from the town. The gas works will draw the soldiers away, so all we have to contend with are the guard-post and sentry patrols. You, Martin, will deal with them. The rest, you have your orders.'

As Martin left the room, Shelagh came up to him. 'Martin please don't go tomorrow.'

'I must, despite everything; I must support my brothers. But after tomorrow night, I'm through.'

'Take me with you,' she pleaded. 'I do not love Kevin, I never have.'

'Come on,' said Martin, 'I'll walk you home.'

As they reached the alley across the road, Shelagh turned to him and, grabbing his collar, pulled his face to hers. He put his hands to her breasts and then down to her thighs, pulling her by the buttocks as he kissed her. He could feel the warmth and the passion raging in him. As suddenly as it had started, he firmly pushed her away. 'I'm sorry Shelagh, but you are Kevin's now, and there is nothing we can do about it.'

The tears flowed from her face. 'Oh! Martin we'll find a way.'

Martin shook his head and walked off into the night, He didn't notice someone in the shadows of the doorway across the street.

The next evening they met together on the outskirts of the docks, Sean passed out the guns, explosives and detonators to David and Jacob. 'Go careful now, you will only have ten minutes after the patrol has passed to lay your charges and get back over the fence. You Carriag, and you Kevin, be careful; you have the furthest to go, so timing is critical. As soon as you hear the gasworks blow, allow three minutes to set your own charges, five minutes to get to the Dock wall, then you, Martin, attack the Guard post. Keep them under fire for about ten minutes, that'll give us chance to get back to the trucks, then covering fire as we make our break for it. Understood?'

'Understood,' came the reply.

David and Jacob were the first to reach the gasworks. As they cut a hole to breech the fence they found themselves surrounded by British soldiers. They had no chance to fight as they had their arms full of explosives. 'Hell and Damnation!

We've been set up.'

Further down, Kevin threw a grappling hook over the Dockyard wall and proceeded to hoist his way up. Out of breath, he finally arrived at the top of the wall, whilst Carriag, below, fastened the explosives to the satchel and signaled 'haul away.'

Suddenly a search light directed its beam on Kevin, and a shot rang out. Kevin gasped and fell back into the Dockyard, Carriag grabbed his machine gun and fired a burst at the search light, extinguishing it.

A voice commanded, 'Drop your weapon or we open fire.'

Carriag fired at the voice and was answered by an immediate burst of return fire, the bullets striking him in the legs.

Meanwhile, Martin was waiting for the explosion when he heard the sounds of gunfire. 'Shit,' he growled, 'they've been discovered.'

Then all the searchlights at the guard post came on at once and soldiers were edging out of the gateway, directing their machine-guns towards them.

'Come on,' Martin yelled, 'we're out of here.' Together they ran back through the alleyways to their trucks.

'What's going on?' Shouted Sean.

'They must have been ready for us,' one of Martin's group shouted back.

'What about the boys?'

'We don't know' Martin said, hollowly, 'but we can't wait. They will be all over us in a minute.'

Two hours later they were seated in the cellar of Sean's house. 'The lads should have been back by now, we are going to have to keep low for a while. Here's some money to get you through the next few weeks. Keep in touch through the grapevine. Ok?'

There was a knock on the front door. They looked at each other. Silently Sean went up the stairs and said to Mary, 'See who that is, it could be the lads. If it's the British they would have kicked the door down.'

Mary opened the door. 'It's Shelagh,' she whispered.

'What the hell are you doing here?' Sean remonstrated angrily, 'The Brits could be here any minute.'

'I saw you come back and came to see if Kevin's alright,' she replied, looking over Sean's shoulder at Martin.

'Come in, girl, quickly now. The lads and Kevin are not back yet. There was some shooting, but we don't know what's happened.'

'We've been set up, that's what,' one of the men from Martin's squad complained bitterly.

Thumping his great hands down on the table, Sean's frustration was apparent to all. 'Shut up and stop being ridiculous, no one knew the set up but us. Right, you have all got your orders; at first light make your way out and get clear out of Wexford,'

As Martin's lads returned to the cellar, Martin turned to his Father and said, 'Dad, I've had enough, I said all along that tonight was a mistake. When I go, I'm not coming back until this war is over.'

'Son, son,' implored Sean, 'it's almost over, the uprising saw to that. A few more months is all we need.'

'I'm sorry dad, mam, but I'm sick of the killing and the bombings. Give my love to David, Jacob and Carriag when they get back. I know we always fight like cats and dogs, but I love them just the same.'

Martin's Mother crossed over to him, her eyes streaming with tears. 'Oh! My little love, take care of yourself darling.'

As Martin walked through the front door, Shelagh followed him. 'Martin, take me with you, please.' She held him tight.

'As long as you and Kevin are together, there is no place for us.'

'But Martin, we're not together any more' she cried.

'What do you mean, girl?'

She stopped herself. 'Nothing I, err, just meant I didn't love him any more.'

Breaking her grip on him, Martin replied, 'Oh! Shelagh, I've loved you more than anyone in my life, but you made your choice. Live with it. Goodbye.' He gave her a brief kiss on he cheek and walked away.

CHAPTER TWENTY-ONE

Shaking his weary head, Martin looked up at the sky again. The moon shone high like a signet ring. He finished the last of his whiskey and said, 'Come on Bracken, time for bed.

Having to rise early in the morning, Ray Morgan locked the farm door, walked over to the fireplace, and raked over the last embers of the logs. Blowing out the lounge candelabra, he lit a candle and checked around the room once more before climbing the stairs. Stopping on the landing he glanced into David's room. He walked over to the bed and gently removed the thumb from David's mouth. A stirring at the bottom of the bed made him look down. 'There you are,' he whispered. From the blankets two gleaming brown eyes looked up at him and Brambles tail wagged slowly as if in beat with his heart.

'Go on then,' Ray said wearily, allowing the dog to remain. He quietly went back to the door, leaving it open a couple of inches.

Walking down the narrow passageway, he carefully opened the door of Heather's room. He felt a little guilty, as if intruding, but it was an innocent paternal feeling that he had for both the children. Heather was fast asleep, lying on her back, the glow from the candle outlining the curve of her breasts that he could see through the flimsy nightdress. Embarrassed he shut the door quickly and went to his own room.

Margaret was asleep, lying on her side with her knees in a foetal position. He snuffed out the candle that was standing on a cupboard, sat on a corner of the bed, and proceeded to undress. Ray always slept naked in bed, to let the night air cool his body. He briefly looked out of the window and drew the curtains, then leaned over and gently kissed his wife on the side of her forehead. Slipping beneath the covers, he leant against the head-board.

Twenty years earlier, he had, as a young man, gone with some friends to the 'young farmers' dance, at Hawkshead. There must have been close on about eighty dancers in the hall, many of whom he knew personally, and some he had courted for a while, but never seriously. His parents expected that some day he would marry a farmer's daughter. Suddenly a crowd of girls arrived. They were all strangers, laughing and giggling merrily as they made their way to the vacant tables.

One in particular caught his eye. He watched her for a while, then as soon as the next dance had finished, he made his way across the room.

'The next dance is the *Yearning Saunter*,' announced the compare.

Arriving at her table, he looked down at her and gently touched her shoulder. As she looked up he smiled and said, 'May I have the pleasure of the dance please?'

Rather conscious of her shortcomings, she answered, 'Oh! I would love to, but I don't know how to do it.'

'Come on,' he offered, 'I'll teach you.'

She rose from the chair and walked onto the floor. He couldn't help but feel his own heart pounding. Gradually she picked up the directions he was giving her, and just about had it right, when the dance finished.

'Thank you, I enjoyed that very much,' he said, before enquiring if she would like to dance again later.

'Yes, she would like to.'

'How about a drink at the bar?'

'Yes please.'

Following her to the bar, he noticed, rather chauvinistically, the line of her buttocks as her hips swung side to side. He loosened his tie, and thought to himself, 'I sure do need that drink.'

As they stood at the bar, they chatted about all the general things an inquisitive couple might ask. Then she dropped a bombshell; she was married. Her husband was an American, working at the base at Flookborough. Some of the girls there had asked her to come with them to the dance, and Tom, her husband, said that, as she was with a crowd, it was all right.

They made polite talk and danced together most of the night before her friends shouted to her, 'come on the van's here.' She gave Ray a light kiss on the cheek and swept way. Turning back she called, 'see you again some time.'

It was to be almost twelve months to the day before they were to meet again. Ray had gone back every Saturday to Hawkshead, and, occasionally, to the mid-week dances at Cark-and-Cartmel. He had given up hope of seeing her again, whoever she was, for he had neglected to ask her name; it didn't seem necessary when they were together.

Ray had been persuaded by his pals to go to the 'Hawkshead Farmers Ball'. Arriving a little late in the evening, he noticed that his two friends had picked up a couple of girls for a quick- step, so went to the bar to order the drinks. As he was reaching into his pocket for some change, he became aware of the smell of Jasmine.

'Its you again then?'

He looked down, and there she was. 'Oh! Hello,' he said, rather lamely. 'Thank you lord,' silently offering a prayer to the heavens. 'Would you like a drink?'

'A glass of cider please.'

'Would you like to sit down?'

They made their way to a vacant table and took a seat. 'It's a long time since you were here.'

'Well yes,' she answered, 'I now live with my parents back at home in Barrow.'

'I don't understand. What happened?'

'Well its not too difficult to explain. Tom didn't like the idea of being a father, it interrupted his affairs, and I do mean 'affairs.'

'I am sorry,' Ray appologised. Then asked, 'what do you mean, being a father?'

'Well after you and I last met, well,' she repeated, blushing. 'Well I was pregnant at the time we last met, though I didn't know it; and when I told Tom some weeks later, he blew up. He hit me and called me names, said he wasn't the father, but he was, he really was. I have never been with anyone else.' She began crying.

Comforting her, Ray said, 'Come on now, its all over.'

Calming down, she went on to explain that she had run away from the camp to stay with her aunt Violet. Though her aunt and uncle were childless they were very kind and supportive, and provided a room for her whilst the baby was born.

'Where is the baby now?'

She began to cry even more.

'Come on,' said Ray,' come outside into the fresh air.'

They walked out onto a veranda and stood by the rail. Wiping her eyes, she explained that the baby had been born with leukemia and had died at three months of age. Her friends at Newby Bridge had persuaded her to come tonight. Honestly though the chance, well it was the thought that you might be here, that swayed me. I hope you don't mind me saying this?' She blushed again.

'Good God, no, laughed Ray. 'I've been coming here for the last year trying to find you, even knowing it would probably be impossible. Do you know, I still do not know your name.'

'Margaret,' she said, 'I have reverted to my maiden name, Margaret Wright.

For the next two months Ray travelled every Friday, Saturday and Sunday night to Walney Island where Margaret was now living with her parents. He took her to the Ritz, the Odeon, the Majestic, the Gaiety, and the Regal cinemas, as well as to dances at the Coliseum. On Sundays they walked the four miles from Vernon Street to the New Inn at Biggar where they played whist.

Eventually Ray took the plunge. Walking with her up to the cliff tops, he asked her to marry him. 'If you don't,' he laughed, 'I will throw myself off.'

She looked up to him, the breeze blowing in her beautiful red hair, and, shouting out to the sea, replied, 'Oh! Darling, I do love you. Yes, Yes, and for all the world to hear, yes.'

Ray took her back to the farm, his elderly mother and father were absolutely delighted. Within six months they were married at Saint Mary's Church on Walney Island. Four months later both his parents died from influenza and they were left on their own to run the farm.

Now, as Ray looked at the sleeping form of his wife, he remembered the heart break when, seven months later, Margaret miscarried and was told that she would never be able to have children again. Ray snuggled down into the bed and put his arm over his wife, cupping her breasts.

She murmured, 'good night darling,' as her hand cupped to that intimate place she knew he liked her to touch most.

CHAPTER TWENTY-TWO

Alter leaving the German agent at the store, Niall headed the fifteen miles of winding coastal roads to Barrow-in-Furness situated on the peninsula and foremost part of Lancashire. Passing through the sleepy hamlet of Grizebeck and over Kirkby moors to Askam, he paused at a small village, about a mile outside the town, to buy some cigarettes. Then, turning down a short cut to by-pass Dalton, he entered Barrow, passing the steel and wire works factories. By the time he arrived at the timber-yard it was mid-morning. He purchased the wood required by his boss, Oliver Clark, to renovate the Hughlock home.

As yet, he had not met Mark, and his thoughts were on the outcome of their meeting, since it would be now six years since they fallen out. He smiled to himself. 'Friendship? No,' he thought, 'we were more like brothers.' In the normal coarse of events he would have given body, life, and sole to both Mark and Jane, but an argument, as they had, with the intensity of the fight and all its pent up emotions, would forever leave a lasting effect. He even held a sort of contempt for his father's actions, as told to him by his Uncle Carriag. Thus he could justify to himself the actions he was about to carry out on his Grandfather's orders.

Leaving the van to be loaded by the timber-yard staff, he removed his bike from the roof rack and cycled along Ferry Road to Old Barrow Island. Two islands, Walney and Barrow, separated Barrow-in-Furness from the sea. Barrow supported a population of about two thousand people, as well as the mighty *Vickers-Armstongs* and *Maxims Marine and Gun Manufacturers*.

Carefully crossing the old tramlines, Niall made his way down to the commercial docks. Despite the war and the war material being built there, there was little in the way of security. Yes indeed, there were army and navy patrols, but they just marched up and down like toy soldiers. Oddly enough the main security came from the Home Guard, the ARP and Air raid Wardens. These were the men who, for the most of them, were in reserved trades, and had been conscripted to do so many hours per day and night to watch over the town. Even Niall had an admiring respect for them, and knew that he must be careful in his actions.

He left his bike in the worker's bike-shed and walked the extra half-mile to the southern end of Ramsden Dock Road. Carefully looking around, he entered Vickers through a hole in the fence behind an old broken shed on the edge of the allotments, an action that he had carried out once a week for nearly eighteen months. Walking through a derelict warehouse that had, many years before, been a chandler's store, he changed into a pair of overalls before entering the main factory site and mingling with the workmen.

Strolling along the dockside, he noticed the destroyed crane and a few lightly damaged sheds. Across the docks, the face of the granary had been badly damaged. 'Well, so much for the Luftwaffe's marksmanship,' thought Niall. He made a mental note of the positions of the two cruisers on the far side of the Devonshire Dock. A submarine with P69 painted on the conning tower was on a slipway and, either side of the next dock, were two aircraft carriers.

Suddenly the factory siren wailed out over the town, and he could see from the Town Hall clock a quarter of a mile away that it was five minutes to twelve, the time when those workers who went home for dinner would, by now, be lining up at the gates. Making his way past the blacksmith's shop, he cut through the joiners and pattern makers, before mingling with about two-hundred workers, some pushing bicycles, some walking, and at the rear, those beginning to kick-start their motor bikes. Again the siren wailed, the gates flew open and a mass exodus of men and women went through onto the main road, Niall amongst them.

Once clear, he made his way to the Crow's Nest Hotel down the road. Entering the tap room, he was met with a cheery, 'Hello Peddlar, cards or dominoes?'

'Not today Tom. I have to get back early, big job on an estate at Ulpha,' he replied with a wave of acknowledgement. As he watched the cards being dealt out, he noticed a handful of submariners by the bar. Walking over, he stood beside them, carefully listening to their conversation, which mainly consisted of humdrum talk about their wives, girlfriends, and children, mingled with the odd humourless joke.

Then one asked, 'Meet the new Commander today, don't we?'

'Aye,' came back the reply, 'sailed with him until last week.

Comes from around here somewhere.'

'This will be his first command,' the other sailor butted in. 'Believe he lost his wife and parents, so I heard, Decent bloke though, should be good trip.'

'You know where we are going, Frank?' asked another.

'No, but it must be special.'

A large Petty officer had come in and stood behind them. 'Best keep your mouths shut or you'll be going nowhere but the brig. Go on, get sat down and keep your traps shut. See those sign's on the wall, 'WALLS HAVE EARS.' He spelt out the words for them.

Niall smiled and went over to the card school. 'See you lads, perhaps time for a game next week.'

Niall wanted to get away before the 12:45 siren sounded its warning for the end of the dinner hour, as he knew he would have a difficult job getting through the crowd of workers from the nearby docks. Returning to the timber-yard, he secured his bike to the roof-rack on his van and went into the office. After signing for the material, he started his journey back to Broughton. Waiting to pull out onto the main road, an official looking black Bentley drove past. Through the window he saw Mark Hughlock, dressed in full Naval uniform, and made up his mind to meet him as soon as possible.

CHAPTER TWENTY-THREE

At eight o'clock that morning at the King's Head, Mark received a telephone call from Naval Headquarters in Portsmouth.

'Mark, are you able to go today to Vickers at Barrow? I know you are in the midst of a difficult period but things are coming to a head and I'm afraid personal problems have to take a back place.'

'Yes, sir,' replied Mark, 'as long as I can make the funeral of my wife and parents tomorrow.'

'Mark. This is very important but we are not that callous. Report to Rear-Admiral Winder. the Naval Attaché, at the Personnel Office, Michaelson Road.'

'I know the place sir.'

'Fine, Mark. Can you make it for one o'clock, they'll send a car for you?'

'Yes Sir,' he replied, saluting.

Descending the stairs, Mark entered the lounge of the pub where breakfast was just being served.

'Morning sir, going anywhere nice today?'

'Well I was going to the church to see Reverend Young, but I have to go into Barrow for lunch time, so I will have to make a few phone calls instead. But first I have to go across to Mr. Clark's to confirm some of the changes I want doing to the house.' Mark and the landlady exchanged a few more pleasantries. As he left to cross the road, a van, driven by

Niall O'Leary, came out of the alleyway at the back of the shop.

'Peddlar. Oh Peddlar,' Mark smiled, and thought to himself, 'I will call on Mara tonight. Maybe if Peddlar's there, we can settle our silly feud. He must know what's happened to Jane, he thought.

His first call was to Oliver Clark, confirming that only repairs to the kitchen should be carried out, as he couldn't yet bear to walk into the conservatory, that was something for the future. He then phoned the Reverend Harold Young, whose wife Evelyn confirmed that Stella had made all the arrangements, and that a small number of friends of his parents had been invited to a reception at the village hall.

Two hours later, his car arrived.

CHAPTER TWENTY-FOUR

Leaving Horst to cook in a bucket what was left of the lamb that they had appropriated from a local farm house, Richter spoke to his colleague. 'Keep a careful eye on that smoke, only use dry wood.'

'Where are you going?' enquired the young airman.

'We have had a good look around this valley, so now I am going to have a look over this mountain. I'll be back in two or three hours. Don't move from here until I get back; understand?'

Yes Obermeister, mien fuhrer,' he replied sarcastically.

Hans Richter did not bother to chastise him; this was hardly the time or place considering the position they were in.

He followed the sheep track over the head of the wood and came out onto an open fell. About a mile or so down into the valley, he could see smoke rising from a farmhouse chimney. Looking back in the direction he had come from he was relieved to see that the smoke from their own fire was obscured by the tall fir trees. Crossing over a small rivulet, he trod carefully through some marshy ground onto the firm base on the fellside. The bracken was quite dense, coming almost up to his neck, though occasionally it cleared into open ground. He stopped and watched as an adder, basking in the early morning sun, slithered into the undergrowth. He shivered slightly and muttered, 'filthy thing.' Continuing along a path that had suddenly appeared in the bracken, he came across a small stream, babbling down the mountainside. A signpost, pointing to a gap in the mountainside, read, 'Walna Scar, Coniston. 3 miles.

Richter looked carefully around. 'No one in sight,' he muttered to himself. Then, taking a deep breath, he climbed over a wall and started up the hillside, glancing back from time to time to assure himself of his solitude. Highs in the sky two ravens were harrying a large buzzard. He watched for a while as they circled, each trying to peck at the buzzard, but it was having none of it, endeavoring to retaliate if they came too close for comfort. Finally, tired of their interference, it flew off over the crags.

After walking for what seemed miles, Richter arrived at the summit of, what had by now become obvious to him, a 'pass.' Though he had seen beautiful sights before in the Bavarian and Austrian Alps, the panorama before him was something special. To his left was a large mountain, not as big as those in the Alps, of course, but just as magnificent. He was delighted by the multitude of colours seen in England's countryside, and even when he was on some of the daylight bombing raids, he was always over awed by the views below him. He glanced up. More ravens were flying across the crags like overgrown bats. Looking down the hillside he noticed a small village nestling in the base of the valley, whilst in the distance, a lake reflected the sunlight that shone on the surrounding hills. Deciding not to proceed further, Richter sat down on a boulder to rest. Looking back in the direction he had come, he could see the sea, and, on the horizon, the Isle-of-Man. The quietness of the area astounded him; even the ravens had stopped screeching, as if they were telling him, 'Ok! You leave us alone and we will leave you alone.'

The sun was getting quite warm, so he took his jacket off and laid it on the ground. Sitting on it, he laid back against the boulder and, in the peace and tranquility, thought about his father. He didn't know why this should suddenly come to mind, just maybe the thought of being so far from the war made things so small and insignificant. His Father was the Luttwaffe's Commandant in Jersey. It was only a few weeks ago that they had occupied it and he had been fortunate in being able to be one of the first bomber pilots to ferry the planes in before returning to Munich. His Father had been an air ace in the First World War serving with 'Immann,' that war's greatest German pilot.

His Father, Ludvic Von Richter, had shown him around the Island and taken him to his headquarters in Elizabeth Castle. There had been no resistance in the taking of the Island, many of the Islanders being quite reasonable in their conduct towards them, and so the occupation hierarchy had allowed the British police to maintain civilian control. The Germans had immediately started to build sea defences, utilising Russian and Polish prisoners-of-war, and were planning an underground hospital in preparation for the invasion of England.

Both he and his Father stayed at the Grand Hotel, where they had two very enjoyable days together, drinking the local beer and sampling 'Ormer,' a shell fish caught at low tide, that tasted like a succulent beef steak. Richter's thoughts turned to his home in the village of Allach, situated some fifteen miles from Munich. He had just started work in the giant 'Krauss-Maffei' factory, which dominated the village, when war broke out. The company made everything from tanks, guns, and agricultural equipment, employing some six thousand people. He was eighteen years old when some of his colleagues took him along to the Martassa Bar, the largest beer hall in Bavaria, on the famous Mariana Platz. It was here that he first saw Herr Hitler. Impressed with his nationalistic views, Richter joined the Luftwaffe on his 19th birthday, since when he has flown on missions over Spain. In 1939 had been transferred to the Bomber squadron at Cologne, but was disappointed in having to exchange the solitude of flying to being in command of an air crew.

Apart from his father, Richter had no other family, his mother having died of tuberculosis many years ago. His initial excitement at being posted to Jersey soon turned to disappointment when he discovered that, at his father's request, delivering spare planes and parts for the Island's Luftwaffe was not to be a permanent position. He had asked his father why, but was not given a reason, other than to obey orders.

Stretching himself, he looked up at the sun directly above him, and suddenly realised that it must be about midday. Hans would be getting nervous. He picked up his jacket and was about to step out from behind the boulder when he noticed a man walking along the hillside.

'Where the hell did he come from?' Concerned that he should not be seen, he watched the man continued down the pass. As soon as he was out of view, Richter made his way along the mountain trail. Coming across a well-worn track leading to a gap in the hillside, he followed it for a while until he came to the entrance of a mine, partially hidden by bracken and shrubs. A corrugated door, secured by a piece of iron rail, was leaning against the entrance. Pushing the door to one side, he cautiously entered, the light from behind him beaming down upon the floor, reflecting on the stones that were strewn about. Struck by their colour, he picked one up and walked back outside to see it in daylight. 'Looks like copper ore,' he thought to himself, 'must be an abandoned copper-mine.

Walking deeper into the mine, the passage bared left. Following the rusty iron rails he came to a table with an oil lamp upon it. Touching the glass, he drew back quickly with a soft curse, for it was quite hot. 'Why should anyone come here?'

Lighting the wick with his cigarette lighter, the flame slowly illuminated the area. He notice a sheepskin on another table. Raising it, he found a suitcase concealed underneath. 'What the devil is this?' he wondered, carefully opening it.

'Oh! Mien Got in Himmel'

There before him was a radio and transmitter, together with a book, which, on opening, he realised was a German codebook. 'The man that I had seen earlier was not Bauer, so who could it be?' He considered his position carefully, before putting the book back in the case and covered it with the blanket. 'Tomorrow,' he thought, 'I will get to the bottom of this; this could be our way home.'

CHAPTER TWENTY-FIVE

Mark entered the Personnel office at the 'Kings Gate.' Passed through the large wrought iron gates embossed with the name, VICKERS ARMSTRONG AND MAXIM LTD., he paused and looked at the open double-doors of the General Machine Shop, observing the lathes, drills, and capstan machines working full out for the war effort. The young girls were working on the bogies, small flat wagons used for trafficking the raw and finished articles from bay to bay.

Climbing the stairs, he rang the bell on the reception desk.

Mrs. Rita Forshaw, the Personnel Secretary, came to him. 'Yes sir,' she enquired in her inimitable high-pitched voice.

'Admiral Winder is expecting me.'

'One minute,' she replied. Returning along the corridor, she stopped and knocked on a door. 'Your one o'clock appointment sir.'

'Oh! Fine,' came the response, 'send the gentleman in.'

Mark was duly escorted into the office. 'Good Morning sir.' Mrs. Forshaw edged her way behind Mark as he saluted the seated officer.

Captain Norman Jewel nodded and returned the salute politely, requesting his visitor to sit down.

'Would you like some tea sir?' she said

'Yes please,' replied Jewel, looking at Mark, 'Two teas, milk and sugar.'

Mark who nodded in agreement. Mrs. Forshaw closed the door behind her.

'Right then Hughloch, you may be puzzled as to why we have sent for you. Before I explain, let me apologise for Admiral Winder's absence. Unfortunately he has been called away and ordered me to fill you in on the situation.' Captain Jewel then opened a draw, extracting a large drawing of a submarine.

'Mark' he said, raising his head from the chart, 'you don't mind me calling you by your first name do you?'

'No sir,' he responded.

'Good. We are a bit informal around here. Right,' he started again, 'this is what we have here.'

Mark looked down at the drawing.

'P 69' H.MS.Seraph Class 1940 S
Displacement: 715 tons surfaced, 990 tons submerged
Dimensions: Length 217 feet, Beam 23ft. 6in., Mean draft 10ft. 6in.
Crew: 44 to 48
Propulsion: 2 sets Admiralty design Diesels (1900 BHP). 2 sets Electric motors (1300 BP)

Armament: 6- 21 in. Bow torpedo tubes
 1 -21 in. Stern tube carrying total 21 torpedoes
 1 –3 m. A.A. gun
 1 – 20 mm Oerlikon Machine gun
Speed: 14.75 Knots surfaced, 9 knots submerged

'Mark,' calling his attention to the crew number, 'this submarine is to be designed for special operations. The work going on at the dockside is of paramount importance and I want you to oversee it. I realise you have personal problems at the moment and we do have a latitude that the submarine has some way to go before completion, but it must be ready for commissioning in three months, and that includes sea trials. This submarine will then be under your full command and until then you will report to me. I cannot make the meeting with Sir Arthur Duckworth that has been arranged for tomorrow at his home; however it is the wish of the Admiralty that you, being the future captain, attend. I can only tell you that it is a feasibility study for an operation to deceive the enemy and to try out new technology for future submarines. So for the next three months you must be extremely careful to whom you talk to. Any questions.'

'No sir,' he replied, 'I look forward to my first command.'

There was a knock at the door and Mrs. Forshaw came in with the tea. 'Fine then Mark, when we have had our tea I will show you where the sub is berthed and introduce you to some of the civilian staff.'

It was about four o'clock in the afternoon when Mark said his farewells to Captain Jewel. The car was waiting for him outside the offices across the road. 'Take me back to my hotel please,' said Mark to the driver, 'and that will be all for today.'

Mark lay back in the rear seat as they made there way out of the town. Instead of going the short cut along the industrial side of the town, they travelled down Abbey Road, reputed to be one of the longest tree lined main roads in the country.

'Got that last night sir,' the driver called over his shoulder as they passed the Municipal Baths, which had been reduced to a load of rubble. 'The Church as well.'

The road had been cleared, but the firemen and ambulance workers were still lifting the rubble. Probably searching for bodies, Mark thought, musing at his own loss. They carried on down the main road to the outskirts of the town. On the right, below them in a valley, he could see the ruins of Furness Abbey, destroyed by Henry VIII during the Reformation. Nearby stood a large, circular, grassed amphitheatre, where locals still carried out open-air theatrical plays.

Driving up to the T-junction in Dalton, they turned right past the *Red Lion*, up the hill to Dalton Castle, then bared right until they reached the summit, where the road narrowed into long winding lanes. The view opened out to the left of him. He could see the Aerodrome at the North end of Walney Island, and, where the runways ended, the expanse of sand hills that camouflaged the gun emplacements. The sea swept around the head of the island, down into the channel, and back into Barrow-in-Furness, like a coiled viper.

Blackcombe mountain could be seen in the distance standing like a dark shroud. It was really an overgrown fell of which Mark, Jane and Niall had climbed many times. Down in the valley, smoke was belching from Millom Iron works. From

Barrow right up the coast to Whitehaven there were industries which seemed so far away from civilisation that Mark often wondered how any of it had come into existence. Shortly after passing Kirkby moors they entered Broughton, coming to a stop outside the hotel. Mark turned to the driver. 'If you fancy a quick drink, see the landlord and put the charge on my tab.'

'Thank you very much sir, all the best.'

After changing into civilian clothes Mark walked across the road to the garage. The owner, Mr. Parfitt, looking up from his office desk, recognising Mark at once.

'Well hello! Master Mark, it's good to see you after all these years, Oh! My condolences on your family loss, you may be sure my wife and I will be there tomorrow.'

'Thank you Mr. Parfitt. The reason I'm here is, well have you got a car I can hire for a week or two, maybe longer?'

'Of course, my young sir. Come round the back.'

Mark walked through the office and out into the backyard where Mr. Parfitt stored a couple of vans, a Bentley and a two-seater M.G.

'Well' said Mark, 'if its all right with you, the M.G. will do me fine. Can you fill her up, here are my petrol ration cards.'

'Already full, Master Mark, the keys are in her. Settle the bill when you are ready.'

'Here's ten pounds on account.'

'That's more than enough,' Parfitt replied.

Mark slotted himself into the car, having adjusted the seat to give himself more leg-room, and drove back to the hotel.

Entering the lobby, he picked up the phone, and placed a penny in the slot.

'Connect me to Ravenglass Mansion please,' he requested of the operator.

'Is Miss Stella Duckworth there?' he enquired.

'One moment sir.' There was a brief wait then Stella came on.

'Stella Duckworth, can I help?'

'Extremely. I am in dire need of female company.'

'Is that you Mark?' she replied, recognising his voice.

'I have a car,' explained Mark. 'How about a spin to Coniston and a bite out?'

'I would love it. It will give us the opportunity to discuss tomorrow's funeral service.'

'See you at seven tonight then.' With a sense of satisfaction, Mark replaced the receiver.

CHAPTER TWENTY-SIX

Niall dropped the timber off at Mr. Clark's warehouse and drove back to the caravan. Bauer, or Thompson, as he had to keep reminding himself, had been in the valley after returning from Barrow, and had ordered Niall to re-set the transmitter up in the mountain, himself being beset with the problem of the mobile units under his command.

Mara kept several antiques in the caravan, together with a couple of beds, a rocking chair, and a sofa. On the grill of an iron fireplace that stood in one corner, a kettle was boiling.

. 'Hi! Stranger,' came a voice from the rocking chair.

'Hi! Dad,' Niall replied, 'tea about ready?'

'I'm surprised you bother to come back at all. It's usually the early hours when you get back. I must get to meet this girl friend of yours.'

Niall laughed. 'One day dad, one day.'

Mara stood up and, from a cupboard, took some eggs, bacon and potatoes. After brewing up he peeled and sliced the potatoes, put the chip pan on the fire, and before long had a meal going for the two of them.

Mara asked, 'are you out tonight then?'

'Aye!' replied Niall, 'I'm off to Coniston.'

'That's where she lives, is it?' laughed his father.

Niall just smiled, poured some whisky into his hip flask, and put on his climbing boots.

'What are you doing?' enquired Mara.

'I'm leaving the van here and walking over the Scar. I want to be in Coniston before dark.' After helping his father with the cleaning up, Niall put on his duffel coat, set off down the valley climbed over the stile, and strode firmly up the fell side. The evening air was crisp and clear as he climbed the fell. Two hours later, arriving at the abandoned mine, he pulled aside the corrugated sheeting and entered. Uncovering the transmitter, he cabled up the antenna and tested the batteries. Being at least three hours away from transmission time he made himself comfortable, then, after taking a drink from his hip-flask, he closed his eyes allowing his mind to wander back to Ireland.

The welcome at his Grandfather's home was like the prodigal return of Joseph, except for Carriag, that is. Though he appeared friendly enough, there always was that air of resentment. His Grandfather Sean owned a fleet of lorries and a successful haulage business, transporting goods to Northern Ireland and England. His sons, David, Jacob, and Carriag, all had their own trawlers and fished around the coasts of Ireland and Isle of Man. once a year they would fish the Icelandic area. Though successful, they lived a modest home life, and as a family they were all very close, with only a select number of friends.

His Grandmother had made up a spare room for him that was both private and comfortable, and for the next two weeks he had lounged about the house during the day and in the evening drank with his Grandfather at Finnagan's Bar. His cousins, David and Brendan, were rarely around as they were both drivers for Sean, but David's girl friend offered to show him about. She had taken him to Cork where he 'kissed' the Blarney stone, and to Waterford to collect some paperwork for Sean

It was after the second week, whilst in County Kerry, that the accident happened. Crossing a ford on the river Dalna, their vehicle struck a boulder that had been swept down during a recent flood.

'Damnation,' cursed Mary, 'that's all we need,' as she and Niall climbed out of the truck to examine the damage. Fortunately a farmer in the opposite field had spotted their plight and offered to fetch his tractor.

Awaiting his return, Mary pulled out a packet of Woodbine from her cardigan pocket. 'Compliments from David on his last trip to England,' she explained. 'Filthy things but they will have to do.'

Niall took two, placed them between his teeth and lit them, returning one to Mary. 'It's going to be dark soon, we'd better find a place to stay.'

Luck was with them for the farmer returned with both the tractor and a local garage owner. Pulling the pick-up out of the river, it was then towed a mile back to the village where, after a cursory inspection, the garage mechanic said he would have it fixed for early morning, and that if they wished, could stay the night in the flat above the garage.

'We'd better phone Sean and tell him where we are, or they will be concerned.'

'Fine,' said Niall.

Leaving Mary to do the phoning, he went upstairs to the flat. To say the least, it was a bit dingy, the double bed lay at one end of the room, there was a couch, two chairs and a table. A small kitchen, used for both cooking and washing, was tucked away round a corner, and the fire was laid but not lit. He put the kettle on and put some tea in a stained brown pot. There were number of cups on a rack and carefully he proceeded to look for two that were not cracked.

Niall heard Mary enter the room behind him. 'Tea?' he called.

'Yes please, one sugar only.'

He smiled, 'No place like home.'

They sat for a while making general small talk. 'Why have you come to Ireland, Niall?'

'Oh! To get away from a mess I was getting into.'

'Girl Trouble?' she enquired, looking at him with interest.

'Sort of.'

'Come on then, tell Mary all about it.'

For some reason that he could not explain, he started to open up with Mary, as if she was a kind of mother figure that he had never had before. Telling her that for many years he had loved a girl called Jane, but knew deep in his heart that she loved his best friend Mark. When Mark told him, just before he was due to go into the Navy, that he and Jane were getting engaged, then for some crazy reason he had exploded, and there had been one hell of a argument with silly and outrageous statements. Then they fought, and in one stupid moment their years of friendship was over.

'No Niall,' Mary responded gently, 'if you sit down and think, friendships do not die, not true friends. Good friends may fight like cats and dogs, but when a friend is like a brother, then, with a little understanding, it will endure.'

'Great counsellor you are, smiled Niall.'

'Come on Niall, there must be more to it than that?'

'I suppose you are right Mary, If I am really true to myself, I think it's because I have never had somebody who really cares for me, except perhaps my Father. My Mother died a year after I was born, Mrs. Hughlock, on whose estate my dad worked, helped him bring me up. But though I loved her, she wasn't my own. I longed for her to put her arms around me and hold me. Funny isn't it, I still feel that way now. I feel that I would burst into tears if some woman ever did that.'

'Niall, you're getting Maudlin.'

'Yes, your right. Well you take the bed and I'll take the couch.'

Mary went over to the bed and took her skirt and cardigan off. She hesitated for a moment, looked at Niall's back, took the rest of her underwear off, and got under the blankets. Niall meanwhile, had lit the fire and pulled the couch within easy reach of the warmth from it.

.'Are you comfortable?' called Mary.

'As well as can be expected,' he replied.

There was a few minutes lull and then, almost dozing off, he felt her arms go round him holding him tight, her breasts pressing into his back. He could not help the tears that poured from him, more tears than he had ever shed as a child. He stood up and turned around, her head came to just above his shoulders, Slowly she unbuttoned his shirt and slid it from his back, running her fingers through the dark hairs of his chest and kissed him on each nipple. Taking her cheeks in his hands, he gently put his lips to hers, not a word was spoken. Mary put her head to his chest. They held each other for a few moments, then, reaching down, she unbuckled the belt of his trousers. His loins were already stirring, the bulge in his briefs pronounced. Kneeling down on the floor, she put her lips to his growing manhood. Her lips ran up and down him till he felt he was going to burst there on the floor. He grabbed her, 'No! Not yet,' he said, then, picking her up, he carried her to the bed and laid her down, kissing her breasts. He ran his tongue down to her thighs and between her legs. Then, in one passionate quick movement, he brought his tongue up her body, between her breasts, before kissing her full red lips. Finally, lying upon her, he gently entered her, and within a short time that he came to a climax.

'Don't leave me yet,' she implored, and a moment later she received a massive explosion that rocked her body. Perspiring, they lay together, until, about an hour later, they made love again.

Early that morning they were awakened by the start of the pick-up truck being driven out of the garage. Niall looked down at Mary. This was the first time he had ever made love and his manhood was rather sore. But he felt like he could walk on water, now that he really new what love was.

He dressed and went to the window. The garage mechanic spotted him and held his thumb up.

'You can say that again mate,' thought Niall.

Gently, he woke Mary. 'Come on Mary, time to go.'

'Come on back to bed 'she yawned.

'I can't,' Niall smiled. Looking down between his legs, he cried out in mock agony, 'I think you have broken it off.'

'Come here, I'll kiss it better,'

'Dress, you hussy, time to get you back home,' slapping her on her bare bottom.

'Ouch, you rotter.' She retaliated by throwing a pillow at him. Getting out of bed, her breasts bouncing as she dressed, Mary looked out of the window and called down to the mechanic. 'What an absolutely fantastic day.'

Niall had never felt so good in all his life. Leaving Mary to wash and replace he make-up, he made his way to the yard. Taking the invoice from the mechanic, he wrote on it, 'Send this to Sean O'Leary's in Wexford.'

'I know Sean well enough to know I'll be paid,' acknowledged the mechanic.

As Mary left the flat she blushed when she noticed they were both watching her smoothing her dress, grinning from ear to ear at her as if their night of love making was clear to see. Throwing them a 'V' sign she stuck out her tongue and shouted, 'Come on Niall, I'll drive.'

The Morning was becoming rather cloudy and soon rain started. 'It looks like it rained heavily during the night as well,' remarked Niall.

'I didn't notice, I was to busy,' she laughed.

They had travelled some forty miles over the hills before arriving at the village of Cahir. Ahead of them, a crowd of people were being held back by the local Garda. As they drew near they saw the wreck of a lorry that had crashed down an embankment, the front cab had been crushed.

'I think its one of Sean's', said Niall, as they slowly edged pass the crowd.

'Oh! God!' Mary shrieked, 'It's David's.' She pulled over to the side of the road and dashed into the crowd.

'Stay back,' ordered one of the policemen.

'It's my fiancé, get out of my way,' she cried, tears streaming down her face.

'I'm sorry miss, there is nothing you can do, and you will

only be in the way.'

A senior officer, seeing the commotion, came up the embankment. 'What's wrong officer?'

'It's this girl sir, claims to be the driver's fiancée.'

'Superintendent Benest, miss. I'm sorry, but the driver was killed instantly. The accident happened about three hours ago, weather was bad. It appears he driving too fast, skidded on the bend, and overturned down the embankment. I really am terribly sorry but there was nothing anyone could do for him.'

Niall put his arm around Mary's shoulder. 'Come on love, leave it to the police.'

Crying bitterly, Mary allowed herself to be taken back to the pick-up, the Police Superintendent followed behind. 'For the record sir, could I have your names, and that of the driver; we will have to inform the next of kin.'

'He didn't have anyone but me. His parents died some years ago and he was lodging at my mother's house. I will tell her, but David worked for Sean O'Leary.'

'All right miss, we shall see to the rest.'

Niall got behind the wheel and drove off.

Mary began crying again. 'What was David doing round here, this is not on his route?'

'Maybe he was coming to find us,' replied Niall, patting her gently on the leg. An hour later they drove into the O'Leary yard. Sean came out of the office as they pulled up. Seeing the tears still in Mary's eyes, Sean said, 'you've heard then?'

Mary nodded.

'Your mother has been told as well. You get home and leave the rest to me.'

Sean gave her a light kiss on the cheek and, as she turned away, Niall called, 'do you want me to come with you?'

'No.' she replied, 'see you later.'

CHAPTER TWENTY-SEVEN

'Come into the office Niall, I need to talk to you.' Sean said tersely.

Niall followed behind, seating himself by Sean's desk. Sean opened a drawer. 'Whisky?' he offered.

'No thanks, too early for me.'

'Perhaps your right, Niall,' Sean hesitated. 'You like it here, don't you?'

'Yes of course, why?'

'For some time now I have been keeping an eye on you. You get on all right with your uncles and your cousins. I have let you do some odd jobs for us, and you have never asked questions. How to you feel about becoming a member of my firm - permanently?' The emphasis was on the 'permanently.'
'Before you answer son, there are something's I shall tell you, stop me at any time, because the further I go into it, the more committed you become, and if you wait too long, the answer will have to be yes. Do you understand.'

'Yes grandfather.'

First, son, you call me Sean.'

Niall nodded.

'Second, your uncles and I do not make a living from just haulage and fishing.'

Niall nodded.

'You know about the 'Troubles' and the 1916 revolution?'

Again Niall nodded. 'Vaguely,' he replied.

'The Irish Republican Army fought tooth and nail for that independence, and, though we have a Southern Ireland, we continue to fight until all Ireland is united.'

Again Niall nodded.

Sean waited a moment. 'Your Father was a part of that continuing struggle.'

Niall looked up, stunned.

'Dad was?'

'Aye, but it got to him and he left in 1921 and went to England. We've met only once since, when your mother and the children died, and that was only at the insistence of your Grandmother. However, to enable our cause to succeed, we smuggle arms and ammunition into the country. Now this is where you have the opportunity to get out, now!'

By this time Niall was so intrigued that he could not wish to do anything but stay. He nodded to his Grandfather. 'Go on.'

'Are you sure?'

Again Niall nodded.

Pausing to take a deep breath, 'Son, I am Commander of all the IRA South of the border, your uncles are all my lieutenants, and Carriag is the Quartermaster, responsible for purchase and distribution of arms. We need a replacement for David, he was very important to us, and as you are not known from the past, your only linkage in this country is through me. Son, what I have now told you is pledged, whether you like it or not, to you. Believe me, should you ever repeat what I have told you out of the circle of people that I will introduce you to, then, even as your Grandfather, I will kill you myself.' The unmistakable threat was followed by a short silence, then Sean went on. 'Niall, do you understand.'

Niall stood up, 'Grandfather,' then correcting himself, 'Sean, I shall be proud to join you.'

Sean shook his hand, 'I reckon we might just have that tot of whisky now. Tonight son we shall all meet upstairs at Finnagan's bar. I shall officially swear you in to our cause, and tell you what I want you to do.'

Raising their glasses, they made a toast: 'To the Island of Ireland, Sinn Fien.'

At nine o'clock in the back room of Finnagan's bar, fifteen men were sitting around a table. To the right of Sean sat Jacob, and on his left, Carriag and his son Brendan. Sean gavelled the table with his tankard of ale.

'Brothers of Ireland,' he called. The murmur in the room ceased. 'Tonight is a sad night for us in the loss of David. Though not in the line of fire, no less a loss to us, for he was a partner in our struggle, and was the young cousin of another who died eighteen years ago during the abortive battle at

Rosslare harbour - none other than Kevin Ryan. Brothers, a toast to David Flaherty.'

They all stood and raised their glasses, 'David Flaherty.'

'Sit Down Brothers. We now come to another serious moment. The loss of David is a bad blow to us and I have decided on his replacement.'

The audience looked toward Sean.

'Brendan, let him in,' pointing at the door of a side room. Brendan passed by the seated men and opened the door and beckoned to Niall. 'You're wanted.'

As Niall entered the room Carriag jumped up. 'What the hell! Martin's son. Never in a month of Sunday's.'

'Shut your mouth Carriag, I give the orders here, and you obey them. Brothers,' turning back to the others, 'this you all know is Niall O'Leary, my Grandson, and the son of a former Brother.'

'Informer more like it,' snarled Carriag.

'None of that,' snapped Sean angrily, 'that charge has never been proved, and I for one will never believe it. Now shut that moaning trap of yours and listen. Niall, when I spoke to you before, you understood the consequences of the actions we are about to take?'

'Yes Grandfather,' Niall nodded.

'Be upstanding, Brothers.' They all rose in obedience to their Commander's call.

'Niall O'Leary, raise you right hand. Do you swear, on this League of United Brothers, for the struggle for the Islands of

Ireland, that you will be obedient to the precepts laid down by your commanding officer's and superiors, to fight for the cause in the capacity called upon, even unto your death, and to protect all who serve with you unto the same.'

'I do,' confirmed the newly initiated Brother.

'Then, Niall O'Leary, you will seal this obligation on the Bible of the Brotherhood.'

Niall took the bible from Brendan and dutifully kissed it.

'Niall O'Leary, you are now a member of the cause. We salute you.'

In one motion the gathering raised their left hands in a clenched fist. Sean came to the foot of the table and shook Niall's hand, and one by one the rest of the assembled men followed in suit, except Carriag, who remained seated.

'Gentlemen, this meeting is now closed. We will adjourn to the bar to toast the memory of our departed Brother, and the introduction to the ranks of our new Brother, my Grandson.'

Patting Niall on the back, they all made their way down the stairs to the bar, where a glass of whiskey was awaiting each of them. Sean called them all to order. 'Gather round lads.'

'To departed friends.'

Knocking their drinks back in one gulp, Sean shouted, 'fill them again Tom,' then, making another toast, 'To our new Brother.'

A voice from the door entrance snarled, 'No traitor's son is a Brother to me.'

Sean called, 'Carriag, I've warned you.'

Before he could say any more Niall stood forward. 'Are you calling my Father a traitor?'

Carriag stepped towards Niall, rage showing in his eyes, 'Your father, yes, he was responsible for Kevin Ryan's death, and through his treachery, both Kevin's and my brothers went to prison for seven years. And then this.' As he tore open his shirt, Niall could see five red scars running across Carriag's stomach. I have as many on my left leg as well, thanks to your father.'

'I know my father too well to know he would never inform on anyone,' shouted Niall, his own temper burning up in him.

'Why do you think he never spoke of us here in Ireland?'

'I do not know, but I will not stand here and allow my father to be defamed by the likes of some bitter and twisted liar.

Carriag raised his head, and sneered, 'What, little man, are you going to do about it,' as he rocked back, laughing.

Niall hit him square on the jaw. Carriag flew back across the room, taking two men down with him. He shook his head. 'You young bugger,' then, rising to his feet, he took a swing at Niall, who, stepping to one side, hit his opponent in a downward punch knocking him the floor again. Carriag got to his feet again, this time forming himself into a boxing crouch, and swung another punch at Niall. Niall ducked and the impetus of the intended blow swung over his shoulder. Niall kicked down on the back of Carriag's leg, bringing him crashing to the floor. Before he was half up Niall struck him behind the ear, and this time his intended assailant did not rise.

'Throw some water on him,' ordered Sean. A tumbler was found and the order carried out. Spluttering, he raised himself on an elbow and smiled at Niall. 'Tricky sod, aren't you? Here, give me a pull up.' Niall smiled back and walked over to him, offering his hand. Taking hold of it, his uncle gave a swing with his other arm, hitting Niall square on the jaw, laying him out cold.

It must have only been a couple of minutes later when he came to. Holding him in her arms was a middle aged woman and behind her looking anxiously was Mary Ryan. Shaking his head, he glanced around; Sean and Carriag were sat with his other uncles on the other side of the room.

'Damn you,' muttered Niall, struggling his feet. Throwing an impeding stool to one side, he began to advance, his fists up.

Carriag watched him coming towards the table. 'Battle's over, we'll call it a draw. You are a game one, I'll say that, no one has knocked me down in many a year.'

Jacob chipped in. 'As I recall, it was Martin.'

Carriag scowled at him.

Niall stopped, and, staring at Carriag, said 'Uncle, I will obey your commands, I will fight your battles, but two things.'

'What's that son?' yawned Carriag, still feeling his own jaw.

'Never in my presence call my father a traitor.'

'And the other?'

'Never hold your hand out to me again.'

'Sit down lad and have a drink.'

A line of whiskey's had been set up at the table and Mary and the other woman came across and joined them.

'This is Shelagh Ryan,' Mary said, introducing her mother. 'Shelagh offered her condolences to all those assembled. I am sorry about David, I really am. It's one of those sad things in these troubled times that we never seem to find an ending. 'It appears that David was coming to find you both for some reason, and lost control of the lorry. Why he should be travelling at such a speed I don't know.'

Niall looked across at Mary, who momentarily turned her head away, as if embarrassed.

'The funeral is tomorrow, so, for tonight, lets just drink to his memory.'

The couple raised their glasses then Mary went and sat by Niall. 'David,' she began to explain, 'was the cousin of Kevin who was killed some years ago. He looked after David until his death, then Mother took him on. At first, when we were kids, we were like brother and sister, but the last few years we seemed to get so close that getting engaged seemed inevitable.' She looked at Niall and said softly,' until yesterday.'

He patted her hand. 'Let's see how things go for a while, we don't want to start upsetting anyone now, besides, I have had enough fighting for one day.' They drank until the early ours of the morning and, as the crowd slowly disappeared, Sean called to his son. 'Jacob, you and Niall, at my house, ten sharp. Ok.'

They both nodded.

As Carriag got up to leave, he smiled at Niall, and waved a salute at him. 'Good scrap eh!' and walked out. Shelagh followed him.

'Are they?' Niall joined his fingers together.

'Well yes,' replied Mary. 'I was born almost nine months to the day from when my father was killed, and it was only twelve months after Carriag had been released from prison that his wife died from pneumonia. They just seemed naturally to come together. Kevin was his best friend and they were together at the wall when Kevin was shot. He died instantly and Carriag was badly wounded.'

'Where did my father come into it?'

'Oh! I don't know, you should ask your Grandfather about it some time. Well,' she said, 'I'd better go , we'll get together this weekend. Bye darling,' she whispered, kissing him on the cheek.

The next morning Niall got out of bed with what could only be described as a breath of living death. The whiskey had taken its toll on him. Crawling across the bedroom, he looked in the mirror and stuck out his tongue. 'Yuck! Death, where is thy sting?'

After a wash and shave, he put on a clean shirt that his grandmother had ironed for him, slipped into his shoes, and glanced around the room as if expecting it to disappear. With a sigh he descended the stairs.

'Want do you want for breakfast, Niall?'

Despite the length of time he had been in Ireland, no one called him by his nickname, 'Peddlar,' and it still made him start to look over his shoulder when called by his Christian name. 'Just coffee, grandma,' he called.

'In here Niall,' the voice of his grandfather boomed from the lounge. He walked in, Sean was sitting in his rocking chair whilst Jacob was seated opposite him, drinking coffee.

'Morning.'

'Morning,' he echoed back.

'Sit down, son,' beckoned Sean. 'Niall, over the next few months I want you to work closely with Jacob on the St. Marie.'

Niall looked puzzled.

'That's one of our trawlers,' explained Jacob.

'I want you to learn about being a radio officer. Jacob will teach you Morse Code. I also want you to learn some basic German as well.'

'Why German?' Niall again looked puzzled.

'Never mind why, just do it without question, ok.'

'Well actually grandfather. Sorry,' said Sean, raising his arm in admonishment, 'I mean Sean. I already know German quite well from my father, he was fluent in it.'

'By God' said Sean, 'I forgot about Martin altogether. Well son, its going to be a case of like father, like son, but don't tell Carriag I said it.'

'Now, today is David's funeral. He had lots of friends and some may not be too happy that he was travelling to meet you and Mary when the accident happened. David was a jealous man, and probably thought that you two were up to no good. So,' he drawled the word out, 'Jacob will be taking a crew of two and heading off to sea, where, in seven days, they will rendezvous with a ship carrying some contraband goods for us. Jacob will fill you in once you are on the ocean. You will be gone for about three weeks so you can also get some experience in trawling. You will find some waterproof clothing in the kitchen. Any questions?'

'No Sean,' replied Jacob, 'I'll get ready now.' Then, turning to Niall, 'meet you at the docks at noon then, Mary can give you a lift down.'

Mary had just come into the room from the kitchen, 'Run you where?'

'To the docks' replied Sean, 'Niall is off with Jacob for three weeks.'

'Oh!' she cried, and with a look of disappointment on her face, walked in a huff back into the kitchen.

'What's up with her.'

Niall shrugged his shoulders. An hour later, arriving at the dockside, he turned to Mary. 'Maybe it's for the best. Let things cool off a bit, but believe me Mary, I think I am in love with you.'

Mary kissed him on the lips. 'Three weeks then, bye darling.'

Niall jumped down from the pick-up and boarded the trawler. Jacob, together with three other members of the crew were already there. 'Niall, let me introduce you to Frank, Bill, and John. Old Charlie is in the wheel house,'

Niall shook hands with his new shipmates.

'Store your gear below and we will get underway. Frank, cast off stern lines, John, cast off bowlines.' The diesel engine roared into life and slowly they edged their way out of the harbour. From the stern of the boat Niall watched Mary waving until they had disappeared around the headland.

CHAPTER TWENTY EIGHT

Over the following eight months, Niall became an expert radio operator. During what little time he had to spare he would send Morse code messages to Jacob or Charlie, by tapping his fingers on the table. Having quickly gained his sea legs, he helped with the hauling and casting of the nets, and it was only on two trips that they had smuggled contraband goods. The first was a delivery of packing cases, about which Jacob never elaborated and Niall didn't ask any questions, whilst the other, cases of brandy and rum. On the end of each trip Jacob would report direct to Sean, but Sean never once talked about the voyage to him.

After each voyage, Niall became closer and closer to Mary until it appeared that there relationship was accepted by all. Nineteen-thirty-nine was half way through and Niall had never been so happy in his life. In another month it would be Mary's birthday when they were to announce their engagement.

Jacob invited Niall to the bar for a drink. 'Niall, we have a special job on. We sail tomorrow.'

'Christ, Jacob, I've arranged to take Mary to Cork for the weekend.'

'Sorry Niall, this is an order direct from Sean. This is a special so cancel your trip, we sail in the morning. We'll be gone for a week. Take care not to talk, not even to Mary, understand?'

Niall nodded miserably, 'I'd better go and tell her that we're off.'

'No! Tell no one. In fact I want you to go down to the boat now and check out the radio, the lads will be there soon. We stop on board until high tide. Sean will tell Mary for you tomorrow.'

Though there were many questions on his mind, Niall thought it better to stay quite. 'How do I get to the docks?'

'Pick your gear up now, my van's outside. Someone will collect it in a short while.'

Obeying his instructions, Niall collected his clothing, and was surprised to find a parcel on the kitchen table.

'Flask of coffee, half a bottle of rum and some sandwiches,' came a call from the lounge.

He went in. Sean was sat in his chair smoking his pipe. 'Go carefully son, go carefully.' He stood up, looked at his grandson, left, and went to bed.

Niall shuddered ominously, and went out to wait for the van. Fifteen minutes later he was on the deck of the boat, making his way to the wheelhouse. After checking the radio transmitter, he went down to the galley, where, illuminated by a candle, a bottle of whiskey and some glasses adorned the table. Stepping into the gloomy shadows, he threw his gear on the floor and placed his parcel on the table. Glancing towards the forward bulkhead he was surprised to see two Thompson machine-guns and four rifles propped against a cupboard. Pouring himself a stiff drink, he was about to lift it to his lips when he heard, 'Pour the same for me.'

Startled, Niall looked into the shadows, immediately recognising Carriag. 'You scared the shit out of me you stupid idiot.'

Carriag laughed. 'Teaches you to be cautious in this job, thought you would have learned that by now, especially with an old man like yours.'

'Carriag, if you're drunk and looking for trouble, this is not the time or place.'

'Trouble is but around the corner, son, and you better be aware of it now. Jacob is not coming tonight, I'm in command so you better be a hot shot on that radio. To be sure, you will not be leaving that set unattended, from two days out until we are in visual contact of our party. In particular you will listen out for Coast Guard, Irish, and Royal Naval transmissions, because, my young fisherman, at eleven o'clock tomorrow night, it's probable that England will be at war with Germany and we will be up shit creek if caught by those three nations, England, Ireland or Germany.'

Over the next three days Niall had hardly slept, the earphones never leaving his head. At eleven o'clock of the first evening, he heard the announcement that Britain was now at war with Germany. Strangely enough his thoughts were not with the war situation, but with Mara, Jane, the Hughlock's, and the friends back home that he hadn't seen for almost two years.

Suddenly, the transmissions started calling, 'Albatross to Seagull, do you read?' being repeated over and over.

'That's us,' shouted Carriag, 'answer back.'

'Seagull to Albatross, we read you strength five.' About two hours later John shouted from the wheelhouse 'Ship off port side.' Half a mile away a small cargo ship was steaming toward them. Carriag left the wheelhouse and handed a machine gun and three of the rifles to the crew.

As the boat came alongside a shout was heard. 'Are you the St. Marie?'

'Yes,' Carriag replied.

'We have your package, do you have our money?'

'Of course. Do you think I am here to sunbathe?'

Another man with a marked Spanish accent joined in, and shouted, 'Come aboard. We shall settle our business quickly.'

'These are troubled waters now,' Carriag shouted back, 'you come here along with your cargo and we shall be on our way.'

Suddenly, one of the covers of a large packing case was thrown off, revealing two men on a mounted machine gun. 'Drop your weapons,' the Spaniard commanded, 'or we will open fire.'

From behind a winch, Charlie fired a shot at one of the machine-gunners, and was cut down by the immediate return of fire.

'You bastards,' shouted Carriag.

'Drop your weapons now or I will sink you.'

'The money will go down with us,' yelled Carriag angrily.

'I think you will float long enough,' sneered the Spaniard.

'Drop your weapons, lads,' shouted Carriag, looking down at the body of Charlie.

The Spaniard, leaping onto the deck of the St. Maria, demanded, 'The money, Captain. Twenty five thousand pounds.'

Carriag, looking up at Niall who was standing behind the cupboard with the other Tommy gun, picked up the briefcase, and nodded at the gun.

'There you are, what about the guns.'

'I'm afraid I have a better offer from your compatriots in the North,' answered the Spaniard, with a nonchalant hunch of his shoulders. As they turned away from the wheelhouse, Niall followed, firing a burst at the two machine-gunners who were now standing at the edge of the boat. They were killed instantly. Another crewman fired back, but Bill had picked up his own rifle and shot him. The Spaniard spun round in surprise and Carriag went for him. Dropping the case of money on the deck, they both grappled each other, plunging them over the side of the trawler.

By now the sea was beginning to get rough and both boats were only about a yard apart. The Spaniard had floated away from Carriag when suddenly the two bows crashed together crushing the Spaniard, his body disappearing beneath the surface. Niall rushed to the trawler's side where he spotted his uncle in the water, struggling to remove his heavy coat.

Running along the deck he shouted, 'Here, before you get caught,' and, leaning over the side, he put out his arm.

Hesitating for just a moment, Carriag smiled and called, 'A hand out to an Irishman?'

Gripping with both hands around his uncles wrists, Niall replied, 'come on you stupid bastard.'

Bill and Niall dragged him on board. Carriag, getting to his feet, looked at his nephew. 'Son, my hand will never be in anger with you again, that I give my word. You saved my life.' They shook hands and held each other round the shoulders.

'Right, lets get this cargo on board.' Bill and John swung a derrick out over the cargo ship whilst Carriag and Niall boarded the Spanish boat. Two hours later they had completed the transfer of eight large packing cases.

'Get back on board, Niall,' ordered Carriag. Soon the trawler was making headway. Looking back, they watched as the stricken ship sank beneath the waves. 'Profitable day, twenty thousand pounds and a full cargo.'

Five days later they arrived back in Wexford, Mary and Sean being at the dockside to meet them. Sean commiserated, 'I'm sorry about old Charlie, he was a good Brother.'

'We buried him at sea,' replied Carriag. 'We'll report it as man overboard to the authorities.'

'Lets get back home then.' The father and son smiled at each other as they watched the young couple walk hand in hand ahead of them. 'Isn't love wonderful?' Sean put his arm around his son, 'perhaps you could take a tip or two from them.'

Arriving at the street where Mary lived, they were alarmed to see an ambulance outside her house. As they ran nearer, Shellagh was being brought out on a stretcher. Niall's grandmother walked towards them. 'Mary dear, its your mother. I found her collapsed on the floor, they're taking her to Wexford Infirmary. You go along with the ambulance.'

It was some hours later that the hospital doctor came to Mary's side. 'Mary, It's cancer of the liver I'm afraid'

'How is she?' concern choking her voice.

'Sedated at the moment, and with suitable painkillers she may go home in a few days.'

'Home! Why home?'

'There is nothing we can do Mary, I'm so very sorry.' Crying softly, she walked with Niall back to the van and got in, sitting for a while without speaking. Then Mary sighed and started up the engine. 'Come on, let's go home.'

Niall's grandmother opened the door. 'I have tidied up the bedroom for you.'

'Thank you, you're very sweet,' Mary acknowledged, 'I'll put the kettle on.'

A few minutes later Sean came in, 'How is Shelagh?' he inquired.

'Not good. Cancer.'

'Oh hell, I'm sorry. She used to be a lovely looking girl, went down hill after loosing Kevin, but you, little darling, were her light and life.' Then, speaking directly to Niall, 'Come across the road son, we need to talk.'

Dutifully, Niall stood up and followed him. He hesitated at the door and turned to Mary and winked, 'See you soon.' Once in Sean's office, be sat down and waited for his grandfather to speak.

'Niall, after what Carriag's said about this last trip, you have a great deal to be proud of. You have shown you have guts and can handle yourself in a difficult situation.' After a short pause he continued, 'Niall, England is now at war with Germany. If Germany had won the last war, all Ireland would now be united and not, as we are now, divided. So the struggle for independence will not be finished until the British have left us for good, and the only way for that to happen quickly is for Germany to win this war. Britain is not prepared, and the war should be over in a year or two at the most. Now son this is the important part. All over the British Isles, they will be working flat out building ships, planes, tanks and guns. Industries will be manufacturing everything for the war effort. Importantly for us is to delay them by any means, and that means sabotaging them wherever we can, and that is where you come in.'

'Me!' exclaimed Niall, 'What can I do?'

'A lot son. Barrow-in-Furness is probably the biggest shipyard in the country. You, having lived in the Lake District, are known to many people, and that gives you access to the town and the docks. I want you to return home and act as our agent, supplying information only. You do not need to do the sabotage work, just prepare the information and transmit it to me by Morse, you are an expert in that field now. I will relay it to the German authorities.'

Niall looked seriously at his Grandfather, 'How long have you been planning this,'

'Son,' said Sean, 'from the day after you arrived.'

'What about Mary? We are getting engaged shortly.'

'No! Wait a while. I'm sorry son, but your only commitment is to our cause, and any interference from your love life could create problems. Son, when this is over you will have all the time in the world for her.'

'But what will I tell her?' his frustration apparent.

'Say your father is unwell, and you have to go back for a short while.'

'When do you want me to leave.'

'In a week,' replied Sean, 'John leaves today to meet up with a German submarine and collect a special long-wave transmitter and codebook. You will have to test it, then one of the boys will take you by boat and slip you into a cove near Millom. Do not mention this to anyone at all.

A week later Mary and Niall stood on the dockside at Wexford. The freedom of Shelagh not being in the next bedroom, they had spent the night together making love. Mary was now sobbing at the thought of their parting.

'You will be all right darling?' asked Niall, showing his concern.

'Of course,' replied Mary, 'mother is coming home tomorrow, and will need constant attention.'

Carriag called from the boat, 'Come on lad, time to go.'

Niall kissed Mary on the lips whilst fondling one of her breasts. He laughed, 'just to remind me what I'm going to be missing.'

She looked tenderly at him. 'Just be sure you don't look any where else.'

Again Carriag shouted. 'Come on, we'll miss the tide.'

CHAPTER TWENTY-NINE

Niall woke with a start and, in the glimmer of the candlelight, looked at his watch. 'Shit!' he exploded, 'that was close; three minutes to midnight. He turned on his transmitter and waited until the hand on his watch reached twelve. 'Peddlar to Romany King, Peddlar to Romany King,' he tapped out. A response came back immediately, and he started to send his message, detailing damage done at the Barrow docks, advising of the new submarines being built, and of the two cruisers on the slipways, almost ready for launching.

'*Package,*' referring to Bauer, '*established locally and will report soon. Extensive activity in area to discover transmitters.*' He then signalled, '*end of transmission.*'

A moment later the acknowledgement came back. '*Have the package with you, same time tomorrow for urgent message. End of transmission.*'

As Niall signed off, he felt a chill down his back. He shuddered again as he shut the case and unhooked the aerial.

'Don't move or I will shoot you.'

Niall's heart pounded as he slowly raised his hands, cursing himself that he wasn't armed. 'So, my friend, you are in touch with Germany?' Niall kept quiet. 'Turn around slowly,' ordered the stranger. Niall edged round on his stool. In the gloom of the candle he could just make out the outline of a man. As the stranger stepped forward into the light, Niall gasped. He was wearing the uniform of a German pilot, around his neck hung a small iron cross, and in his hand, pointing directly at Niall's chest, a Luger automatic pistol.

'You're German?'

'Of course,' was the reply.

'Where did you come from?' Niall asked nervously.

'We crashed in the hillside a few days ago.'

'This must be the bomber that hit the house,' thought Niall, angrily, rising from the stool. 'You bastard, you killed innocent civilians down there.'

'Sit down now or I will add one more to the list, besides, what are you talking about, we discharged our last bomb to get over the mountain.'

'Well mate!' snarled Niall, 'You killed my friends.'

'I'm sorry. Fortunes of war do not separate the good from the bad.'

'Do not patronise me you sod. Who are you?'

'Oberleutenent Hans Von Richter at your service.' He attempted to click his heels but only succeeded in putting up a cloud of dust. 'To Business my young friend, I think you are both mine and my compatriots ticket out of here. Would your package happen to be Major Bauer?'

Niall hesitated. 'What do you know of him?'

'Well, for a start it was him who let the bomb loose on your friends. He jumped out before we crashed, but we were so low that I thought he might not have made it.'

'Who else is with you?' asked Niall.

'My young navigator. He is, I think, back at the aircraft, probably playing with himself,' he replied, smiling, and allowing Niall to lower his arms; though with the gun still pointing at his chest

'Where did you crash?' asked Niall.

'On the hillside down the valley. We were extremely fortunate as the crash loosened the slate, absorbing the impact. We slid down into the top of a forest, the slate covered the side and top of the plane, which, together with the all the trees, completely camouflaged us.'

'Now to business. Can you get us out of here?' a concerned edge coming to his voice.

'Firstly I must report this to Bauer, he is operating as the village policeman.'

'How did he achieve that?' came the surprised response.

'I don't know and I didn't ask,' replied Niall. 'I will contact him today, but I cannot transmit until tonight. Meet me here, but be careful, walkers use this pass during the day.

'Richter lowered the gun. 'Your name I take it is Peddlar?'

Niall nodded.

'How do you think you can get us out of here?'

'Possibly by Trawler to Southern Ireland, but that is not my decision, there are other priorities you understand.

The German nodded, 'We however cannot remain here forever, understand? Believe me, Herr Peddlar, the longer we are here, the more dangerous is our predicament, so we must have a plan to escape.'

Niall agreed, 'I have an idea, but, Bauer must approve it. I will get some clothes and food to you tomorrow night. Today everyone is occupied with a funeral. Wait at least an hour after I have gone before making your way back. And' nodding to the weapon 'you can put that gun away.'

'Until tomorrow then.'

CHAPTER THIRTY

At ten-thirty that morning, Constables Basset and Wordsworth were directing traffic to the small parking places in the village of Seathwaite, a place consisting of just a few cottages, one pub and a general post office-cum-grocery store. Ida Sykes, the area post office van driver, was busy chatting on the shop steps to all that passed by.

'Come on Ida, move your van, traffic is beginning to congest and will get worse shortly.'

Acknowledging P.C. Wordsworth with a friendly wave, she threw the bundle of letters into the rear of her van, reversed into the alleyway, and sped off in the direction of Ulpha. A hundred yards down the road, the Reverend Harold Young was busy arranging the wreaths that had been arriving all morning.

'Where is young David?' he moaned to his wife, 'He promised he would be here to help.'

As he spoke, David rode in through the wrought iron gates on the bike he had borrowed from his uncle. Sorry I'm late.'

'You'd better lower that seat before you kill yourself,' advised the vicar.

'Right place for it, isn't it?' was the smart-Alec reply.

'Now don't you be cheeky; get in there and help Mrs. Young put out the Bibles and song-sheets.'

Even in summer the interior of the church was very cold, yet David loved the place, it had a peace and tranquillity that even in his young years he found very comforting. The solid oak roof-beams, the wall-plaques and the numerous figurines had been admired by worshipers for nearly four hundred years when the ancestors of the Hughlock family had been given the land and titles of Seathwaite for fighting against the Scots. To David it was as beautiful as St Mary's on Walney Island, and he was determined that when he grew up he was going to be Bishop of all the Lakes.

Stella Duckworth entered the door of the church and called, 'Evelyn, are you there?'

'Yes dear, over here,' her reply echoing through the crypt. Stella walked down the aisle with some bouquets of flowers. 'Oh!' cried Evelyn, 'aren't they gorgeous? Another hour and we will be ready.'

'Fine, you are doing a wonderful job.

'Stella, this is David,' she said, introducing Ray and Margaret's nephew. 'He is here with his sister to help at the farm until this nasty war is over.'

'Hello David,' said Stella, shaking his hand firmly.

'Hello,' he responded, 'nice to meet you.'

'David, would you come over to the Village Hall and help me put out the chairs and tables for the guests who will be arriving after the funeral. There will not be that many because most of the men have a meeting on at Ulpha Lodge.'

'Fine, Miss Duckworth,' he answered.

'Call me Stella.'

He blushed and followed her across the road.

CHAPTER THIRTY-ONE

Mark was up early. After breakfast at the inn he placed his uniform and a clean shirt that the landlady had ironed for him in a holdall and drove the short journey home. Entering the hallway, he put his bag down, and noticed that, even in the last couple of days, the house had been cleaned from top to bottom. He passed through the library and into the lobby, where Mr. Clark had made a temporary wood-panelled partition, separating it from the kitchen. He opened the door and glanced in. Everything was now boxed in to keep the rain off and allow the workmen to begin restoration. He returned to the Library and climbed the stairs to his bedroom. Nothing had changed, except that it was now immaculately clean. He threw his gear on the bed and went back downstairs and out into the grounds. Walking down the hillside and passing the rhododendrons, he noticed Mara's caravan, smoke busily puffing from its chimney. As he drew near, Bramble raced towards him. 'Hold on. Bramble,' he laughed, 'glad I didn't put my uniform on with you around.'

Mara came to the door, 'thought it might be you; tea's on the boil, unless you want something stronger.'

'Too early for me, Mara, tea will do fine.'

'Come on in son, surprise for you.'

Mark entered, and, as he did so, Niall stood up from his chair. There was a moment's silence, then, simultaneously, they put their arms around each other and held tight.

'Christ mate, its good to see you again.'

'You too,' replied Mark, his eyes brimming up with the emotion that he had been fighting to hold back for days. Composing himself, he sat down. 'Are you coming to the funeral?' he asked.

'Wouldn't miss it for the world, I loved them all, you know that.' replied Niall, as if expecting some sort of comment, but Mark just shook his shoulder, and said, 'Peddlar, we both did. So what have you been doing with your self then?'

'Oh! This and that, travelled around for a while, then went to see my grandfather and uncles in Ireland.'

Mara looked up sharply.

'We haven't had much time for talking, I suppose, this last twelve months,' Niall went on to explain. 'I was busy with Mr. Clark and,' before he could continue, Mara butted in.

'And you're courting in Coniston. Well, maybe its time we sat down and had a good heart to heart chat like we used to.'

'Well, for my part' said Mark, 'I would love it but I have to get ready, the cortege is stopping here to pick me up at eleven-fifteen. Look, there is a something to eat and drink across at the Village hall, and then I have to leave with Sir

Arthur Duckworth and Superintendent Moses. Some big-wigs from London are flying in this morning to talk about,' he checked himself. 'oh, never mind, its all shop any way.'

'War business?' enquired Peddlar.

'Sort of,' laughed Mark, a little uncomfortably. 'Right, see you later, or if not, a few drinks in the pub tonight.'

'That's Fine. Is it all right if I bring a friend?'

'Sure, of course, male or female?' enquired Mark.

'Male, Sergeant Thompson.'

'I have already met him,' Mark called back, as he left the caravan. 'Seems a nice fellow, I think he's at the meeting this afternoon. I'll tell him if you want.'

'Sure,' smiled Peddlar, 'that would be great.'

Mark walked back to the house; there was a small Standard Eight saloon car outside.

'There you are,' called Stella, coming to the front door, 'I thought you had done a runner.'

'I wish I could,' he replied. 'I shall just slip upstairs and get ready, help yourself to a drink from the cabinet.' Ten minutes later he was back down again.

Stella, still waiting, said quietly and solemnly, 'Mark, the cortege is outside.'

With his cap under his left arm he walked out into the sunlight. The rays shone down through the Elm trees at the front of the house and onto the cortege. The front funeral car, bearing a single coffin, was bedecked with lilies-of-the-valley in the shape of his wife's name, Jane. He looked long and hard, trying not to let the grief pour out, then walked to the second car that carried the coffins of his mother and father. This hearse was covered in carnations and lilacs. He placed his hands on top of the car and broke into un-controllable sobbing.

Meanwhile, Mara and Peddlar had driven up the rise. Peddlar, on seeing Mark in such despair, got out of his car and came and shook him gently by the shoulders. Throwing their arms around each other, Peddlar said, touchingly, 'I'm with you Pal.'

Mark got into the third car with the Duckworths, whilst Mara and his son drove off ahead to get to the church in advance. Almost as a token of remembrance for his parents and his wife, Mark waved at the house. Slowly they drove down the lane; a slight breeze bending the trees as if in homage. At a steady run of fifteen miles an hour the car followed the meandering course of the river Duddon below them, whilst high to the right stood Stickle Pike and the fells of Caw. Carrying on up to Dunnerdale, they arrived at the sleepy village of Seathwaite where cars were parked either side of the narrow road. Constable Bill Wordsworth stepped out and guided the cortege to the front.

Lining the road alongside the cottages, the locals stood with heads bowed. Many had known the Hughloch's all their lives. As they passed the Pheasant Inn, three old men stood up from the bench, doffing their caps, an act that caused Mark to gulp. With a sympathetic smile, Lady Duckworth leaned forward and touched his arm. The cars stopped at the gates of the Church, where the Reverend Young was waiting to meet them. Many of the congregation were standing in the glorious sunshine that had now broken through the clouds over Dow Crags.

The mourners alighted from there respective cars whilst the undertakers prepared to lift the caskets out. Sir Arthur took his wife on into the church. She suffered greatly from osteoarthritis and only with assistance could she walk to the place set for her at the front of the aisle. Mara and Peddlar, standing either side of the great oak doors, nodded in salute as the coffins passed them.

The coffins were set in a triangle, Jane in front and her in-laws behind. The organist began to play Brahm's lullaby as Reverend Young welcomed all those who had come, not only in respect of those sadly killed in the abominable air raid, but those who had come to support Mark in his hour of grief and despair. Songs of praise were carried out and Sir Arthur made a poignant eulogy. Soon the music sounded for the end of the ceremony.

Leading the way, the vicar and the choir lead Mark and his immediate guest mourners to the crypt where the family tomb lay open. The Bearers lifted the coffins onto three stone alcoves and carefully placed them into position. Mark stood for a few moments, then, and with a sad farewell, saluted each coffin and left.

Walking out into the sunlight he waited for the rest of the congregation to follow. As they did, they lined up respectfully, waiting their turn to shake his hand.

In the background Mara tugged Peddlar's sleeve and nodded towards the rear of the graveyard. Walking down the narrow path, they came to a large Yew tree, underneath which lay the gravestone of Peddlar's mother and sisters who had died so many years before. Standing with their caps in hand, Mara leaned his head towards his son, saying quietly and with great sincerity, 'This is a beautiful country, son, with many fine people. You and I owe a lot to them. People like the Hughlocks, well, some may mock them because they were wealthy, but they gave us a fine living, and it was only God's wish that they joined him before we were ready to let them go. It is a scar on any ones soul to bring hurt to these people and this small land.'

Peddlar kept his head down, the tears forming in his eyes, 'I know, Dad, I know.'

Mara patted him on the shoulder, 'Come on son, it's an emotional time for all.'

By the time they had returned to the church, most of the congregation had melted away, those left were heading towards the village hall. Then Peddlar noticed Bauer with the Chief Superintendent. Saluting the Superintendent, the German turned and walked towards Peddlar.

Under his breath Niall said, 'tonight, Kings Head. Very important.'

Bauer nodded, 'I will be there at six o'clock.

CHAPTER THIRTY-TWO

Breaking away from all the small talk at the village hall, Mark strolled up to Sir Arthur who was in conversation with the Inspector. 'Right, what time is this meeting supposed to take place?' he enquired.

'About two p.m. Sir,' Arthur replied, 'there will be you, me,

Moses here, the Sergeant, and two others.'

'Who?' asked Mark.

'Our visitors are flying in to Walney about now. Hush! Hush! You know. Tell you when we get to your house.'

'Fine, but why my home? In the mess it's in, surely your place would have been better.'

'No. It's too open to staff and bye-passers, and it's important that as few persons know as necessary.'

At one o'clock that afternoon, Wing Commander Basil Embrey signalled to the control tower of Walney aerodrome that they were on approach. Landing smoothly, the Blenheim 1V taxied to the far end of the runway where, from out of the dunes, appeared a limousine, it's windows darkened.

Embrey got out first then waited whilst his two passengers alighted. As they entered the car he stood aside, giving a smart salute. By the time the car had travelled one hundred yards, Embrey was back in the plane, signalling his departure to the tower.

Forty-five minutes later the car pulled onto the forecourt of Ulpha Lodge. Looking around, the eldest of the two went up to the Police Officer who had been waiting to greet him.

'A little early are we?'

'No sir, refreshments are inside. The party will be hear shortly, and the grounds are secure.'

'I didn't see any of you chaps as we drove in,' remarked the elder visitor.

'I would have had their guts for garters, Sir, if you had.'

The visitor laughed and took his companion into the Library at the side of the main dining room.

Making their excuses for leaving the funeral early, and being assured by Stella that all was in order, Mark, Moses, and the slightly nervous 'Thompson,' got into the Bentley and were driven back to Ulpha Lodge. Entering the driveway, Mark glimpsed Mara and Peddlar down in the meadow. They appeared to be talking to two men, both of whom were dressed in shooting clothes and carrying shotguns.

Mark and his colleagues parked at the side of the limousine. Nearby, two men, each holding a pair of Alsation dogs, were standing next to a Bedford van.

On entering the house, Mark and his companions were met by Inspector Moses who made the introductions. 'Mark, this is the Commissioner, Sir Michael Lewry of Scotland Yard. Sir Michael, this is Sir Arthur Duckworth, and your host Lieutenant Sir Mark Hughlock, and Sergeant Thompson of the Intelligence Service. Shall we go in?'

Sir Michael led the way into the Library. 'Gentlemen let me introduce you to Lord Mountbatten and the Duke of Kent.'

Mark suppressed his surprise at their presence. 'Welcome to my home, Gentlemen,' then, correcting himself, he immediately saluted.

'No formalities gentlemen. I'm afraid we have to get down to business quickly.

The First Lord took command at the top table chair. The others followed suit, seating themselves around the large dining table. 'As I was saying, Gentlemen. To the point.' Turning to Thompson, he asked, 'have you located the transmissions yet?'

Thinking quickly, the bogus policeman said, 'Not quite, Sir, but we have narrowed it down to the hills above Seathwaite. I have accurate ordnance maps and I need a pretence of a search that in itself would not divert suspicion.'

Mark Interupted. 'Sir, may I make a suggestion?'

'Certainly. Go on.'

'In this part of the country we have hound trailing; that is, a young farmer lays a trail of aniseed across the fells, the hounds are let loose, later to be collected by there owners. We could arrange with some of the locals to mix with your officers,' he said, pointedly looking at Moses. 'Some to follow the hounds and some to look for a hiding place. I would suggest, however, that the most likely hiding places in the hills are some caves and a lot of abandoned copper mines.'

'Can you arrange that at once?'

'Yes Sir, my father's gillie, Mara O'Leary, and his son know the hills like the back of their hands.'

Thompson smiled and made his own contribution. 'Sir, if I may say so, that is an excellent idea. Meanwhile I will have my two constables out with the patrol vans in case of any other transmissions.'

'Give us three days to organise,' said Mark.

'Terrific, well done. I leave that to you Sergeant, liaize with Mark. Now you, Mark, how's the Seraph coming on?'

Mark looked somewhat surprised. 'The Seraph sir, well she is being fitted out now and should be ready in about two months.'

'You have three weeks,' Mountbatten said quietly, 'can you

do it?'

'I will do my best sir. May I ask the reason for the urgency.'

'The reason, which I must add should never leave this room, is that in three weeks, William here, pointing at the Duke of Kent, will be escorting the Dutch Royal Family to Canada.'

'In the Seraph sir?' asked Mark in amazement.

'Yes, that is why this submarine is being fitted with all kinds of detection and surveillance equipment, designed at Sir Arthur's factories. The 'Family,' pointing his fingers in inverted comma's, 'will be staying at Sir Arthur's, details of collection will be given at the earliest opportunity. It is extremely important, as you will no doubt agree, that this information does not reach the enemy. The capture or destruction of this family could wipe the heart out of Holland and subsequently our own country. That is why I have come here myself to underpin that anxiety. Now that you are all in the picture, you can see the importance of taking out this agent, as well as that of completing your project, Mark. The security of the 'Family' whilst at Ravenglass, will be in the hands of your Police Superintendent. That only leaves the problem of how we get the 'Family' onto the Submarine,' mused Mountbatten.

'A small boat could pick them up off the coast of Ravenglass, Sir,' suggested Mark.

'Good Idea, I'll think about that in the coming weeks, they cannot leave via the Barrow docks as they would undoubtedly be seen. Leave that with me for now. Right gentlemen, you have you orders. Good luck, I'm afraid I must depart now, the plane returns at five o'clock. The Duke will remain at Sir Arthur's for a while, as, in his official capacity, he will be examining Barrow's bomb damage. Mark!

Mark stood up and saluted. 'Sir.'

'Mark,' he repeated, 'I wish to thank you for the hospitality and use of your home under these trying circumstances, and you have both mine and my wife's utmost sympathies and condolences for the tragic loss of your family. You have now, I believe, assumed the title of your father, and I am sure you will uphold the traditions of a proud name.'

Mountbatten returned the salute and shook hands all around.

'I shall escort you to your car, Sir,' said Sir Michael.

They all walked out to the drive in front of the house where Mountbatten's car was waiting, the naval chauffeur saluted dutifully, and with a last wave they departed. A moment later another Limousine arrived to collect Sir Michael, Superintendent Moses, and Sir Arthur, the latter turning to Mark. 'Come to dinner tomorrow night, Lady Duckworth would like you to come, she didn't get much time to talk to you at the church.'

'Thank you sir,' Mark responded, 'and I would wish to thank you and especially Stella for all your support.'

As the car drove off, Thompson spoke to Mark. 'Well, they have all got their lifts, looks like I'll have to hitch a ride in the van.'

'No,' laughed Mark, 'come on in and have a drink, then I'll run you down to the King's Head. I'd like to meet up with an old pal of mine, Niall O'Leary.'

An hour later they arrived at the inn. Mark excused himself and said they would meet up again in a couple of hours.

Thompson nodded and walked across to the police station. Basset and Wordsworth were already back from Seathwaite.

'Anything to report?' enquired Bauer.

'There has been a break in at the post office in Seathwaite whilst the funeral was taking place.'

'Much taken.'

'Tins of food mainly, as well as cigarettes, matches, and packets of tea,' Basset replied.

Wordsworth chipped in; 'I reckon its campers or gypsies.'

'Why, have you seen any about?' queried Bauer.

'No Sarg.'

'Well keep your eyes open, its obvious you didn't in the village.'

'Blimey Sarg, with all the traffic and parking going on they could have pinched the church and we wouldn't have noticed,' complained Bassett.

'Precisely! Now to business; at eleven o'clock tomorrow morning I want you both in the office for a meeting on how we can sweep the hills for this so called foreign agent. No need to take the cars out tonight, but you,' nodding at Bassett, 'can follow up this burglary at the post office, and,' pointing at the other officer, 'you can patrol the roads, keeping your eye out for strangers, but be back for eleven.'

CHAPTER THIRTY-THREE

It was almost eight o'clock when Bauer arrived at the King's Head, having had a meal at the Manor Inn. He needed the space to get his thoughts together, and, as yet, had not had the chance to talk to O'Leary. But now, with this new picture of the Dutch Royal's, he had to think of something. Finishing his meal he walked to the Kings Head, where, on entering, he heard Niall's voice calling him.

'Peter, over here.' Both O'Leary and Mark were sitting in a small alcove, alleviating problems of being overheard.

'Sorry I'm late,' he apologised.

'That's ok, I haven't been here that long myself. They chatted idly away for a while, inquiring cordially where Thompson originated from. He concocted a story up about London, but didn't attempt to elaborate, and both he and Niall managed to switch the conversation over to Mark's career in the Navy.

He told them of his time in Fareham, and a cottage he had bought at Locks Heath. Before long, but trying not to give Niall to much information regarding the security that had been discussed at the Lodge, Mark broached the subject of a hound trail. 'Peddlar, over the next three days I would like you to organise a hound trail from Coniston and Walna Scar over Dow Crags. There will be a number of guests, and I would like the local farmers to be present. In memory of my family I am putting up a trophy and a five pound prize for the winner.'

'Ok, sure. But why the rush and why there? There are plenty of better routes,' queried Niall.

'That is not your problem. This is a serious request, can you do as I ask?'

Niall pondered, 'I shall have to ask for some time off from Mr. Clark'

'Any problem there, see me,' ordered Mark. 'He has a large contract with me to repair the Lodge.'

'I still don't see...' Niall tried to continue, but Thompson put his hand on Niall's leg, and stared him in the face.

'Niall, it's important.'

Bemused, Niall could only nod his head. 'Ok, I'll begin first thing in the morning.'

Mark stood up to go to the toilet. 'Beer's going right through me tonight.'

As he left the bar, Thompson said quietly to Niall, 'We have to meet later on.'

Niall nodded, 'I've been wanting to talk to you all day, we have problems.'

'What do you mean?' the last thing Thompson wanted was to be compromised.

'Your German mates are on the mountain.

Thompson could not stifle his shock. 'What!' Several people in the bar looked around, and then quietly went back to their drinks.

'I will explain later.'

'That's a load off my mind,' said Mark, returning. Then, nodding at the almost empty glasses, 'same again?'

A short while later 'last orders' was called. A moan went up from the bar. 'Come on gentlemen,' said the landlord, 'get those dominoes cleared. We close in ten minutes and you know what the police are like round here.'

Thompson looked a little bemused, especially as everyone had turned round to look at him.

Mark smiled at Thompson, 'Nice to be a popular policeman, isn't it.'

His drinking companion acknowledged the humour by raising his glass to all.

Later that night, as Niall and Thompson were driving through Seathwaite, Niall explained the appearance of the pilot, Richter.

'So Richter and his Navigator managed to survive then,' Thompson interrupted with a grin. 'Stelmach, yes, I remember, the other was killed in the raid.'

Richter said you dropped the bomb that hit Mark's house. Is that true?'

'Did I. Well I'm sorry, but I cannot bring them back. All right?'

Niall was upset at Thompson's apparent lack of compassion. Observing this, Thompson snarled, 'Look, there is a war on and you are part of it, and just as involved as I am. And remember,' poking Niall in the chest with his finger, 'we can both hang if we are caught; me as a spy, and you as a traitor.'

Gasping at the venom in Bauer's voice, the word traitor had never entered into Niall's thinking before. 'Richter will be at the mine tonight. He wants to meet you to discuss a way out of the district.'

'No,' he contridicted, an idea already fermenting in his mind, 'tell him I will be there tomorrow.' He had spotted a police car parked by the post office, Wordsworth was talking to a motorist. 'Drop me off here. Tell Richter that we will arrange to get him and Stelmach away soon.'

Niall stopped him as he was about to alight the car. 'I already have an idea that I want to talk to you about.'

'Not now. I have some idea's of my own,' said Bauer. 'Tell me tomorrow.' Bauer then waved at Wordsworth, 'See you tomorrow, goodnight.'

Niall drove the extra two miles or so, past the Morgan farm, and parked in a lay-by. He opened the boot of the car, taking out several tins of food, a number of sweaters, some old shirts, and two loaves of bread. Piling them into a rucksack he began rummaging around in the boot before finding a large jar of coffee that must have fallen out. Securing the rucksack he crossed the road and made his way up the fells. The rain was beginning to fall and the visibility was not too good, but he had walked this path so many times before and could have done it blindfolded anyway. Some of the streams that he had to cross were beginning to swell, making his journey longer than expected. He soon realised that he would not meet the twelve o'clock transmission time. Arriving at the entrance to the mine, he noticed that the corrugated cover had been pulled to one side. 'Richter must be waiting.' He thought to himself.

Moving cautiously into the entrance, he could see the flickering of the lamp in the distance reflecting the copper pyrites in the roof of the mine. As he crossed to the table, two figures came out of the shadow, the elder one called, 'You are late.'

'The time of my arrival has nothing to do with you, and as far as I am concerned you are an unwelcome hindrance,' he replied, sharply.

'A hindrance that, if not satisfactorily helped, could be the death of you,' snarled Richter, not used to being spoken to by underlings, as he perceived the Irishman.

Ignoring his implied threat, Niall asked him, 'Is this your navigator?'

Yes,' he replied, calming himself before he answered. 'Let me introduce you to Oberfeldwebel Horst Stelmach.

Niall nodded. 'Call me Peddlar, no title.'

The airman brought the pleasantries to a close by demanding, 'have you brought any food and clothing, we are wet through, and sick of sheep?'

Niall smiled. 'Yes, I suppose it is a bit lonely out in the wilds,'

Puzzled by a lack of knowledge of British humour, Richter said sharply, 'What do you mean?'

'Nothing that matters,' replied Niall, 'there's food and clothes in the rucksack.

Richter, speaking in German, ordered Stelamch to take some of the sweaters out of the rucksack. Replacing their wet garments, they put their tunics back on top. 'That's a little better. Now Peddlar, how do we get out of here?'

Niall leaned against a wall. 'Tomorrow night I will return and transmit a message requesting my contacts in Ireland to send a trawler to a small port about seven miles from here. We shall then get you either back to Ireland or arrange for you to be picked up by a submarine. But,' he cautioned, 'this is on the approval of people in higher authority.'

'How long do you think this will take?' Richter asked.

'If all is approved, three to four days.'

'How do we get to the coast?'

'I will collect you at a place on a map that I will give you at our next meeting in two night's time. Now,' said Niall, taking out his pocketknife and handing it to Stelmach, 'I suggest you eat some of this food. Here is a knife to open the tins. I must leave now, there is a lot of work to be done in the morning. Take care walking back down the mountain.'

'Peddlar, we have cows in Germany that would eat these mole hills.'

Ignoring the German he smiled to himself. 'Break your ruddy necks then.'

Having left them to carry on eating. he arrived back at the caravan a couple of hours later. Mara stirred in his bed, 'Son, that girl's going to be the death of you.'

'Go to sleep Dad.'

'Goodnight son.'

By now the two Germans had left the mine and were traipsing through the wet mist. As they were crossing a fast flowing stream, Stelmach heard a curse behind him. Turning round he saw his companion was sitting in the middle of the water holding his ankle. 'Shisse,' he groaned, 'I have twisted my foot; give me a hand.'

Stelmach scrambled back into the water and Richter put his

arm around his shoulders for support. 'At least its not far to the plane, I should be ok in the morning.'

CHAPTER THIRTY-FOUR

Mara woke up early in the next day and called to Niall, 'Breakfast up son.'

Niall got out of the bed and looked at himself in the mirror.

Mara called from the kitchen, 'What have you on for today?'

'I have to go round to Coniston, Torver, and Broughton, drumming up support for a hound trail that will be taking place in three days time,' Niall replied.

'Why so soon?' asked Mara.

'Mark has to go back to the Navy soon, and he wants to present a cup and a five pound cash prize.'

If you like, I can cover all the farmers from Ray Morgans, back up through Seathwaite Fells across to Ulpha,' offered his father.

'That's great, dad. That will save me a day's travelling.'

Mara dished out the eggs and bacon. 'Who are you seeing at Coniston?'

'Clifford Tomblin, game-keeper of Lord McGowan,' Niall replied.

'Will you ask him how many day-old pheasants he wants this

year, or does he want to wait until July for them.'

Fine, I'll see to it dad.'

Finishing his breakfast, Niall went to the front of the caravan where a cauldron of hot water was boiling on the fire. Dipping into it with a jug, he filled a basin and proceeded to wash and shave himself. Returning to the caravan he pulled on a sweater and took some money from a small cash box. 'Right dad, see you tonight.'

Mara came to the door and watched his son get into the van and drive away.

Mark was also up early that morning, arriving at the Shipyard long before the early morning rush. Reporting to the gatehouse, he was given his security papers that were waiting for him and escorted down to the offices across from where the 'Seraph' was being fitted out. He followed the civilian office boy up the narrow stairs of the rate-fixer's office and along the corridor. The boy opened the door, 'This is yours, I believe sir.'

'Thank you son,' offering him sixpence.

'Gee! Thanks sir, anything you want, ring the gatehouse and ask for Jimmy.'

'Mark laughed, 'Sure thing.'

It was another hour before two naval ratings walked straight in the office, 'Crikey, Sir!' Coming smartly to attention, 'Leading seamen Higgingson and Howarth sir.'

'At ease, sailors,' replied Mark, returning their salute. Sorting himself at the desk he turned to his two assistants siting before him.

'This submarine has to be completed in three weeks.'

'Three weeks?' they both cried out together.'

Mark smiled. 'Three weeks gentlemen, I want you to introduce me to the managers and head foremen who are responsible for the work. A meeting is to be arranged for eleven o'clock this morning.'

'A bit short notice for this crowd at Barrow sir, they have their tea break about then,'

'Sailor, when I say eleven I mean eleven. One of you, bring your gear to work tomorrow as one will be on night shift, the other will be on days. You can toss up for it.'

'Sir!' Saluting again they about-faced and left the office. 'Blimey,' moaned leading seaman Howarth, 'a right Admiral we've got here.'

At eleven precisely, Mark's office was packed with managers, head-foremen from the fitters and gun-shop, joiners, pattern makers, and sheet-metal workers. A few minutes later the electronics and armament supervisors arrived. Mark proceeded to inform them of the urgency of the situation that made it imperative to have the boat fitted out within three weeks. 'The order had come from the highest authority,' he said.

'And who would that be Sir,' one of the managers chipped in.

'Lord Mountbatten and the Prime Minister. Is that high enough for you?'

'Yes sir, but we will need to take on extra staff from other departments, and overtime and night-shift will have to be arranged. Only the Managing Director can order that on this scale.

Mark pushed a piece of paper with the heading *Vickers Armstrong and Maxim* emblazoned on it.

To all departments,

Lieutenant Hughlock is to receive all due co-operation from all departments to what ever is required to complete the Seraph in time which includes man power, working practices, and hours of working. Bonuses to be offered to all workmen on completion of project.

Lieutenant Hughlock in sole authority

Signed, Sir Leonard Redshaw, Managing Director.

'Will that suffice?'

'Yes sir,' they replied, almost in unison.

'Let me tell you gentlemen, I want a flowchart of work processed to date, and one taking us to its completion in three weeks from today. Please liaise with my two seamen and myself, Daily progress meetings at eleven o'clock each day. That's all, thank you. Now, may I have a conducted tour of the vessel?'

It was twelve o'clock, the lunchtime siren sounded, and all dispersed out of the office for dinner break. Mark sighed. 'After dinner then,' and smiled as they all walked out, fully satisfied with the mornings work. He knew that these men who worked here had hearts of oak, as of Elizabethan days, and was confident that the work would be completed. His main worry was this 'damned' agent who was obviously targeting the Furness docks for bombing raids, and hoped the security in the civilian police force was sufficient to disguise the forthcoming arrival of the Dutch Royal Family.

CHAPTER THIRTY-FIVE

Towering above Coniston, a main centre for ramblers and visitors to the Lake District, stands the 2672 ft mountain known as Coniston Old Man. A number of terraced houses overlook the lake on which so many men had tried to capture land speed records. Coniston is an Anglo Saxon name for King's village and is renowned as the 'Jewel of the Lakes.' John Ruskin had lived just a few miles away, and when he died, he chose to be buried at Coniston, rather than Westminster Abbey.

Inland duck and pheasant shooting still takes place within the ancient forests and hunting grounds that surround the lake, whilst on the moors, grouse is bred for sport. People from as far away as Newcastle or Norwich came to watch hound trailing and fox hunting, the biggest sporting events in the area. Congregating in local Inns, they sang shanties of John Peel and other great huntsmen who had gone before. The Coniston, Patterdale, Lowther, and Ulleswater hunts were but just a few that were scattered over fell and crag.

Niall sat in the *Church Inn* at Coniston, waiting for Clifford Tomblin, the Coniston Hunt Master and head game-keeper for Lord McGowan, to arrive. Close on fifty years now, Tomblin had been brought up with game and hunting and knew every nook and cranny of the hills and vales. His father had been a gamekeeper before him on the same estate, and his uncles had worked the copper and lead mines in the mountains. Tomblin's only fault was his exaggerations in all he saw, only slight embellishments of the truth as he saw it, but he was a character that everyone loved and respected, even when he was at his grouchiest.

'Pint Clifford?'

'Aye lad, thanks.'

'How's the hunt doing this year?' Niall asked idly.

'Brilliant, must have had two hundred foxes up to now.'

Niall smiled. He knew that the hunt had been withheld due to Lord McGowan being away in the war somewhere.

'Dad wants to know how many pheasant you'll be wanting. Day olds or month olds?'

'About two thousand. Month olds,' replied the gamekeeper.

'Two thousand,' Niall said with exaggerated amazement. 'There'll be only a small shoot this year.'

'Oh! All right, one thousand. Serve your dad right if he's bred too many.'

'Dad knows what he's doing,' laughed Niall.

'Sorry to here about the Hughlock tragedy. Couldn't make the funeral, had the tree surgeons in at the south of the estate. Hiring some of the German prisoners to cut them down next month.'

'German prisoners?' Niall looked puzzled.

'Aye, from Grisedale Forest P.O.W. camp, Good cheap labour, they love it and no one ever tries to escape. Food's too good for them, besides it's a cushy life away from Hitler's war.'

'Another pint?' Raising his empty pot.

'Aye lad. Thanks.'

One thing about Clifford was his short arms and long pockets when it came to buying his round.

As he waited for the ale to be pulled, Niall looked around. By the open window some dozen cyclists were sitting around a large oak table, drinking mineral water or tea from their flasks, and eating packed sandwiches.

'Bloody lot,' moaned the landlord, as he handed Niall his change, 'never make my fortune out of them.'

Niall smiled and walked back over to the gamekeeper.

'Yes, Cliff,' speaking with more familiarity now, 'Mark sends his best regards to you and your wife, but my main purpose in being here is to meet you.'

Tomblin butted in. 'I wondered when you would get round to what you wanted. Dad's pheasants?' he chided.

'It's regarding a hound trail.'

'Too early for hound trails, snow still on top of *The Old Man*.

'I know,' Niall was getting to be a bit chewed off with Tomblins' gruffness, 'Mark has put up a cup and five pound prize for the winner.'

'Ruddy hell, that's almost a years salary,' chuntered the keeper.

'Problem is, he wants the trail to be done in three day's time.'

'Three day's? Can't be done.'

'Yes it can, and it will. Just needs a bit of effort on everyone's part. Dad's talking to the farmers on our side of the hill, I'm going up to Torver now, and we would like you to get this side of the hill done.'

'Can't be done,' repeated the old keeper.

'Then flipping well don't do it,' Niall replied angrily, whilst getting up from the table.

Don't fret yourself, lad. You're getting all of a dither. If young Master Mark wants his trail he shall have it.' Then, holding up his glass, 'Another pint?'

'Very kind of you Mr. Tomblin.'

The old fellow scowled and muttered to himself, 'Cheeky young pup.'

It took a further three pints before Niall could extract himself from the gamekeeper's presence, and get to the Torver Inn for a meeting with their local huntsman. As Niall departed, Tomblin strolled over to the bar. 'Landlord, double whisky.'

The innkeeper muttered under his breath 'Tight old goat, hope the next fox bites his balls off.'

The day went well. Niall got the affirmation he required that the hunt would be ready in three days. Meanwhile, Mara had got all the local farmers to agree. Niall and Mara discussed the details of the event at the *Pheasant Inn* at Seathwaite, Niall informing the landlord that he should expect some fifty or more customers requiring pies and peas after the hunt has finished.

Mara then went back to the estate and Niall went in search of Bauer, calling at the police station on the way to let the young constable know about the hound-trail.

'Where's the Sergeant?'

'Back in his hotel room, but should be here shortly. Sorry I can't stop, I'm off down to Seathwaite post office, they have found a button on the floor that might belong to the burglar. Funny design on it they say. If you want the Sergeant, nip over the road or wait here, suit yourself.'

Niall thought for a moment, 'Well there isn't really anything to report, other than the hound trail being confirmed,' so, smiling politely, he said, 'Ok constable, I'll see him tomorrow. Just pass the message on.'

CHAPTER THIRTY-SIX

Shelagh coughed and brought up some phlegm, spitting it into the cup. Mary carefully wiped her mouth for her. 'Come on mam, you will be all right soon.'

'No, Mary darling, please go and get the priest for me and then Calliag.'

'Oh! Mam,' tears returning to her eyes.'

'Don't cry my love, I know when my time's come, and I must make my confession to the Father, and to Calliag.'

'To Calliag mother. What confession do you need to make to him?'

'Darling its something that 1 have held in my heart for over twenty years, now do as I ask you. Now hurry, darling.'

Twenty minutes later the priest arrived.

'Well, Shelagh, it's God's time coming, is it?'

'Indeed it is father, take my confession.'

Listening intensely to Shelagh, the priest began to cover his eyes in horror and disbelief as she told him of the scar on her soul, a scar that she had carried for nearly twenty years. She told him of the affair with Martin and how he had said that, after the raid, he would be leaving her forever. Martin had then kissed her, and the warmth of her body against his only made him more certain that she could no longer be a place in his life. She had made her bed to lie with Kevin.

'After a final embrace, Martin left me. I was crying when I noticed that Kevin had been observing us from the shadows. I tried to run, but he locked the door, then, grabbing me by the hair, he threw me into the foyer.'

The priest sat silently.

'Kevin was in a terrible rage,' continued Shelagh. 'He started to hit me with his hand, then removed his belt and beat my whole body with the buckle. I was screaming at him to stop, but he continued, then ..' she paused.

'In your own time,' said the priest.

'He... He tore off my clothes and raped me.' She sat quietly, tears running down her face as she recalled the memory.

The priest held her hands in his as she continued.

'After Kevin left, I crawled to the window. I don't know why. I felt degraded and wanted to crawl into a hole. I noticed O'Leary passing by. 'Bastards the lot of them I hope they all rot in hell.' I thought. Then the idea came to me.

She paused as the priest looked deeply into her eyes, wondering what was coming next.

'I went back upstairs and removed two floorboards. I removed a piece of rolled-up carpet and carefully unwrapped it. It contained a sniper's rifle that I had often used on missions for the IRA. I checked that it was already loaded and placed it behind the door.'

She felt the priest's hands tighten.

'I cleaned myself up, then walked down to the telephone box by the post office. I phoned Rosslare Garda. 'Listen, and listen carefully, I will not repeat this,' I said. Shelagh hesitated and then continued. 'Midnight tonight, IRA raid on gas works and explosives warehouse. Two men on gas works, two men on warehouse. Entrance over Smeaton Street wall, and group diversionary attack on main gatehouse.'

'After they acknowledged my message, I put the receiver down and returned home,' she told the priest, extracting her hands from his as he squeezed harder and harder. 'Now, my brave son,' I thought, 'let's see you get out of this.'

'At ten o'clock that evening, I took the rifle and crossed the street to O'Leary's Haulage yard. All was quiet, so I removed the keys of the van from the office. Within forty minutes, I had parked the van three streets away from the docks and had walked to Smeaton Street nearby. I entered one of the derelict houses.'

'I know them,' interrupted the priest, in an effort to break the tension.

Ignoring him, Shelagh continued. 'Treading carefully, I climbed the broken staircase, and found a room that overlooked the dock wall. About an hour later I heard the first of the O'Leary lorries. Two men jumped out, the lorry continuing on it's way to the Gas works. Then the second arrived and parked in the street. I knew that Martin's group would be arriving at the dock entrance in the third wagon. Even in the dim night light I recognised Kevin in his familiar Balaclava. I watched as he and Carriag gathered a rope ladder and grappling hook. Calliag threw the grappling hook over the wall and Kevin began to climb, carrying a haversack of dynamite with him He stretched himself on reaching the top and looked around. That's when I shot him.'

'My God,' cried the priest, crossing himself, 'what am I hearing?'

'I knew Kevin was dead before Kevin did. I watched as Calliagh looked up, as a call to surrender came from nearby. I watched as he began to shoot, and saw him fall to the ground. I sat in that room until the area had become quiet again, hid the rifle under my shawl and made my way cautiously back to the van. I was home in less than an hour. I sat down and waited. Any emotion I might have felt for Kevin was now gone for good.'

The priest crossed himself and looked down on the thin form of Shelagh. 'You poor girl. May God forgive you, and may God forgive the soul of Kevin.'

'Father!'

'Yes child.'

'Is Calliag outside?'

'I believe so.'

'Please ask him to come in.'

The priest walked out of the room. Calliag and Mary jumped up from their chairs.

'Not you Mary,' he said softly, 'It's Calliag she wants to talk to first.'

Entering the bedroom, Calliag sat on the chair next to Shelagh, and took hold of her hand.

'Its all right me darling, I'm here.'

With a voice that was now becoming a whisper, Shelagh beckoned him down so he could hear what she had been holding back for twenty years. As he listened, tears came to his eyes for the shame he felt for the rape and violation she had endured in Kevin's attack on her. She repeated the story of how she had revenged herself. At first he could not comprehend; he himself had lived through numerous affairs and intrigues, even co-habiting with Shelagh. After all, when a man's best friend is killed, his wife should be cared for, but to do what Kevin had done to her was pure depravity. It was only when she began to confess about the betrayal of him and the group that his eyes began to lighten with anger. He stood up and walked around the room to compose himself, then sat down again on the bed. 'Go on, Shelagh,' he said softly.

She explained how she had taken the rifle, set up Kevin in her sights, and coolly shot him. Calliag's face contorted with anger, he grabbed her by her shift and thrust his face into hers. 'You traitorous woman, you killed my best friend. You informed on us.' He spat the words out. 'I was crippled in prison for nigh on six years, and held a hatred of my brother for twenty years for something that I thought, all that time, he was responsible for.' His voice no longer under control, 'You vile whore! You have the effrontery to ask for absolution, well Shelagh Ryan, God may give you it, but I never shall.'

He shoved her back onto her pillow, her light fragile frame bounced on the bed tossing her hair like a spiders web. With the frustration and anger that he felt blowing his mind he stormed out of the room, stormed past the two people waiting outside, and slammed the door behind him. Mary and the priest walked slowly into the bedroom and knelt beside the dying woman.

As if trying to rid himself of a nightmare, Calliag walked furiously across the road, entering the public house opposite. Standing at the bar, a voice came from the cellar, 'We're closed. Come back in an hour.'

'Its me, Calliag' he replied.

'It can be the Pope for all I care, we're closed.'

Calliag went to the other side of the bar, took a bottle of whiskey off the shelf, and grabbed a glass from under the counter. Filling it to the brim, he knocked it down in one swig then re-filled it again. A few minutes later, having now sat down at a table with the remaining contents of the bottle, Mary came in.

'She's gone. Calliag, I'm so sorry.'

He growled at her, 'Damn her soul, the only good thing in her life was you, and that had to be born out of a rape.'

'I know Calliag, I've known for almost three years now.'

He looked up at her. 'Darling Mary, I've loved you as almost my own for twenty years, but as far as your mother is concerned, and what she has done to me and my family, I hope she rots in hell. Now for you own good, leave me be.'

Mary put her hand on his shoulder and kissed his cheek. 'God will forgive her, in time you will.'

'Go woman, go,' he cried, choking on his words.

Mary turned and walked out.

'What the hell are you doing?'

Calliag did not even look up.

'I told you we are closed,' the Landlord shouted as he went to grab the bottle of whisky.

'Touch it and I'll drive you through that wall,' grunted Calliag, pointing to the front door.

'Stuff you, Calliag, it's my licence that's at stake.'

Taking hold of the bottle, Calliag jumped up, spun the landlord around and hit him. Years of penned up emotion came at once to the surface. The landlord was flung across the room, bursting open the door. As he fell into the street a Garda patrol car passed by. Two policemen jumped out of their vehicle and raced in. There was a moment's silence, then one Garda, followed by the other, came flying out to join the hapless innkeeper. Within minutes the street was full of locals standing around, assisting the three stricken men.

Sean walked through the door. 'What the hell is going on Calliag?'

'Get out of here, or you will have the same.' The bottle of whisky was empty and Calliag walked over to the bar and took another from the shelf.

'Come on son, this is not like you.'

Calliag turned, sneering at his father. 'Like me, how do you know what I'm like? Go away and leave me alone.' He poured himself another tumbler of the spirit.

In the background Sean could hear the sirens of more Garda cars on their way. 'Come on son, its time to leave, we have more important business to attend to.'

'For Christ sake, are you deaf. I told you to piss off.'

Sean looked over his shoulder, the patrol cars were pulling up outside. 'Oh! stuff this,' he said, and picked up the empty whiskey bottle, hit Calliag over the head. Leaning over the unconscious form of his son, he took a swift drink from the bottle himself, heaved his son onto his shoulders, and departed the inn by the back door.

The front door opened very slowly as a frightened young policeman peered in 'Thank Christ he's gone, he's the last one I would want to tangle with, what with three broken jaws lying outside.'

Two hours later Calliag woke up, looked around, and figured that he must be in his boat. With a head that was throbbing like a Doxford diesel engine and a huge bump on his head, he tried to remember how he got there. Then his father came out of the galley carrying a large jug of black coffee.

'Get some of this down you.'

'Did you hit me or something?' Calliag asked, touching his head gently.

'No. You fell over an empty bottle,' smiled Sean. 'Drink this and. when you have sobered up, there is a job that needs doing. At least it will keep you away from Wexford for a week or so.'

After he had drunk most of the pot, Calliag went into the galley and washed and shaved, the memory of the morning slowly coming back to him. He went back to his father and told him of the events that led to his drunken outburst.

His father listened intently. 'You and the lads have suffered badly by what Shelagh did. I could understand it, her killing Kevin, but why turn you all in?'

'It was to get back at Martin as well' Calliagh replied, 'he had told her that because she was with Kevin, it wasn't right for them to start an affair, and he was leaving her any way. This last twenty years I have blamed all that has happened at Martins door. I've hated him and would have killed him, even though he was my brother. I understand him now when he says our cause is a scar on our souls.'

'The Cause,' said Sean sharply, 'is not a scar, it's a crusade for freedom. The scars are on the English who occupy us, and the sooner the Germans get this war finished, the quicker we'll get the freedom of self rule. Then we'll have no such notions of scars. Martin's scar is that he ran away from his obligation to me, to you, your brothers, and all those that fight for freedom.' Sean said angrily, his body rising with the emotion of his outburst.

'Dad, I realise now that Marlin was part of our cause, he played his role, but he didn't like the indiscriminate bombing, he believed there was no honour in that kind of war.' For once Carriag was trying to justify his brother's behaviour. 'War is not honourable, the only honour is how you die and who you die for.'

'Enough of this, I have no more time for semantics. Like I said, I have a job for you. I want you to get explosives, detonators, sniper rifles and ammunition from the depot and ship them to England. Be ready in two days when I shall have more instructions for you.'

'Where in England?' asked Calliag.

'To Niall's,' he replied, 'and Martins.'

CHAPTER THIRTY-SEVEN

'Happy birthday to you, happy birthday to you.' Heather had come down stairs to a tumultuous welcome from her brother. Running towards her, he gave her a hug, shouting, 'here is my present, open it, go on open it.'

'Hang on David,' she laughed gleefully, 'let me open my eyes first.'

Uncle Ray and Aunt Margaret stood by the table, each with a present and a birthday card, waiting patiently for her to open David's. 'Happy birthday darling.'

'Your mam and dad's birthday gifts and cards are on the lounge table.'

'Oh! Thank you all,' she cried excitedly, 'you are all so wonderful'

'Well today's your sixteenth birthday, eh!' replied Ray. 'Young woman now, you'll be getting married before we know it.'

'Whished!' grimaced his wife, 'don't tease her on her birthday.'

'Me! Tease her. Wait until she sees what you have bought her.'

Mystified, Heather opened the parcel and blushed, hiding it from view.

'Come on,' shouted David, 'what is it?'

'Never you mind.' Heather hastily covered the bra that her aunt bad given her.

'Give it to me love, I'll take it up stairs till later.'

Opening her uncle's gift, 'Oh! Lovely, a pair of hiking boots. Thank you so much.'

'What about mine?' said David, feeling a bit left out of the merriment.

Giving him a kiss on the cheek, Heather replied, 'David, socks for my boots are just what I need. Thank you.'

'Away you soppy thing,' cried David, wiping his cheek with the back of his hand.

Walking into the lounge, she opened the presents from her parents; a polo neck sweater and a pair of nylons. 'Aunt, just look at these.' Heather becoming so overwhelmed that she began to cry.

'What's up with you?' David took her arm, looking concerned for his sister.

'It's nothing, David, It's just that I am so happy. But I do miss mam and dad and the others.'

'Don't worry darling, the war will soon be over and the Germans will stop bombing Barrow. Then you can go home.'

'That's the trouble as well, because I will miss you both just as much.'

Ray patted her on the shoulder, 'Come on get your breakfast. Then you can give me a hand with the cows.'

'Not today, Ray,' shouted his wife, 'It's her birthday, David can help.'

'Thank you aunt, but I don't mind,' Heather said, 'I love it here on the farm and one day I'm going to marry a farmer too.'

The sun came high over the hills causing a number of rainbows to shine down the valley. 'Isn't it Beautiful uncle.'

Her uncle smiled, 'a pot of gold under each rainbow's end, just for you.'

His niece started singing *'Somewhere over the Rainbow.'* Ray smiled and thought hard to himself. 'If only,' he sighed.

From the kitchen window, Margaret could see them both together, and sighed to her self, 'If only.'

CHAPTER THIRTY-EIGHT

Richter was laid up with his swollen leg. Although the swelling had gone down a little from the night before, it was still painful for him to move amongst the rocks and boulders. 'Get some water,' he had ordered Horst Stelmach, 'and we'll finish these tins of soup. Then I want you to go up to the mine to meet this Peddlar and Bauer. So hurry, before anyone is about.'

After filling one of the soup cans with water, Horst looked around him, and made his way to the other side of the river. Climbing through the deep bracken, he came to a small clearing where he took off his shirt and tunic and lay in the sun. Just as he was closing his eyes he heard a shot. Peering carefully in the direction of the sound, he looked down the valley, where, some four or five hundred yards below, a man was turning the body of a fox. Horst watched as the man cut off the fox's tail before burying its carcass under some rocks. Grabbing his shirt, the German edged his way back to the clearance, and ran down the hill. Suddenly he realised that he had left his tunic behind. 'Damn,' he muttered, and, cursing again, turned to go back. Then, thinking better of it, 'Blast! There's no time, I may be seen. I'll get it later on, no one will find it in that thick undergrowth.' He picked up his can of water and made his way back to their hideout in the woods.

Ray, called his dog. 'Can you smell it too, Bramble, there's a fox lying about here somewhere. Bramble jumped over the stile and the farmer followed. They were weaving their way along the side of a a dry-stone wall when Bramble suddenly stopped, his right front paw raised like a pointer.

Ray had just slipped the safety-catch off his gun when, about thirty feet away from them, the fox broke cover. Placing the gun to his shoulder he followed the run of the fox for a couple of yards then fired. Bramble ran up to the animal, sniffed it and looked up as if to say, 'didn't we do well.'

'Good lad,' praised Ray, patting his dog fondly. He took out his sheath knife and cut off the brush. 'Come on old friend, I'll bury this vermin later,' and covered it from the scavenging crows with some rocks. He looked up as Bramble growled. 'What is it fella?' said Ray, searching the horizon with the sun in his eyes, 'Is this bugger's mate about?' He walked up the hill and looked around. The river Duddon ran below, and he had a clear view of the woods to his left and the fell side on one edge of the wood. 'Nothing about mate,' he said resigningly. He turned, but the dog had disappeared.

'Bramble,' he called. There was a short bark to his left, and as Ray made his way through the bracken to the clearing, he discovered the hound sniffing at what appeared to be a dirty grey jacket. He went to investigate. 'Give it here lad. Bloody hell.' A German Eagle was emblazoned on the coat. He checked the pockets, some French Francs and a Deutchemark. 'Bloody hell!' he swore again. He looked around. 'Come on old son, this is for the police to check out.'

They walked at a brisk rate down the hill, back to the farm. Putting his gun back in the kitchen cupboard, he shouted to Margaret, 'Just going into Broughton, be back in a couple of hours.'

'Stay out of the pubs,' came the response, 'We are having a birthday tea for Heather.'

Ray didn't bother to reply. He went across to the barn and hitched his pony, Mabel, to the carriage and set off at a brisk trot.

The German imposter, 'Thompson', was talking to Niall O'Leary by the side of the road in Broughton Square, when Ray pulled up along side them.

'Whoa ! Mabel,' he shouted, bringing the horse to a halt. Grabbing the tunic he dismounted the carriage. 'Sergeant Thompson isn't it?'

Bauer looked puzzled, and turned to Niall, shrugging.

Ray Morgan, local farmer,' said Niall, introducing them.

Aye! Just the man I'm looking for.'

'What can I do for you Mr. Morgan?'

'It's this here,' shoving the tunic at him, 'German isn't it?'

'Looks like it. Where did you get it?' queried Thompson, examining the article.

'A couple of miles from my farm, foot of Dove Crag. Lying in the Bracken.'

'Probably dropped off a plane or something,' said Niall.

'Don't be daft,' admonished the farmer, 'Its bone dry. Dirty yes, but bone dry.' he repeated. 'If it had been there a while it would have been soaked through, you ought to know that Niall.'

Niall wished he had kept his mouth shut.

'You're right, Mr. Morgan, leave it with me, I'll organise a search of the hills. We have a hound trail over there tomorrow and we can keep an eye open at the same time.'

'All right, Thompson, its your business, but with my potatoes being dug up and the odd chicken going missing, I don't believe that it was foxes that got them. I wouldn't be surprised if it's an escapee from Grizedale prison camp.'

'I'll check on that to as soon as I can.'

'Right, I'll see thee.'

As soon as the farmer had driven away in his carriage, Bauer turned to Niall. 'The stupid fools, now every one will know that there is someone up there.'

'What are you going to do,' asked Niall.

'Maybe this is a blessing in disguise,' mused the German.

'What do you mean?'

'Moses and Duckworth are looking for a German agent. Let's give them one, or even two.'

Niall was even more puzzled, 'I'm not with you.'

'Look Niall, when you go up to the mine tonight, take some food with you. Tell the pilot and his little friend to stay there until tomorrow night because the woods are going to be searched.'

'And then what?' enquired Niall, even more puzzled.

Thompson gave Niall the German's tunic. 'When you lay the hound-trail tomorrow morning, drag this up the Fellside.'

'Christ, what do you want to do that for, that would take them direct to the mine.'

'Quiet you fool.' Then, making sure no one was close enough to hear, 'Precisely. The British want to capture agents and their transmitter, we give them Richter and Stelmach as well as the transmitter. Then we have them off our backs long enough to finish our business.'

'But they may give us away as well,' complained Niall.

'Not dead they won't. You do as you are told and leave the rest to me. Can you get me a rifle?'

Niall nodded.

'Do that, and get it to me as soon as possible. When are the explosives due?'

'The day after tomorrow,' he replied. 'I will meet the boat in Whitehaven; it is arriving under the pretext of an engine failure. The explosives will be brought ashore with the engine, and I will hide them on the estate.'

'Is the hound trail now organised?'

'Yes, every thing has come together very well,' replied Niall.

'Make sure you call at the inn tonight with the firearm.' Thompson waited until Peddlar had left and then went back into the police station, feeling quite pleased with himself. The situation was perfect, but he knew his days would now be numbered, for if his scheme to use the German air crew as bait was successful, there would no longer be any need for him to remain in Broughton, 'So things had better get moving fast.'

CHAPTER THIRTY-NINE

The back door of 14 Abercorn Street flew open, caught by a gust of wind. Norman Pearce wearily got up from his chair and closed it. Perhaps, he thought, it was an omen for the days to come. Ever since the bombing at the docks, things had gone wrong. He had fired a shot from his rifle at a passing aircraft, and was now on a 'charge' for unauthorised use of a firearm. He had had an argument with Rita Forshaw at the Church Inn in Coniston, just because she had brought bacon sandwiches. He hated bacon sandwiches. Then his wife, Violet, shouted from the kitchen, 'Are you riding today, Norman?'

'Yes dear,' he sighed to himself.

'Who are you with today?'

'Just some of the lads, dear.'

'I'll have your sandwiches ready soon.'

'Yes dear.' Brushing down the cushions where he had been seated, he sighed again and went upstairs, changing into his tartan shirt and plus-fours. His uniform for that night was already laid out for him, and again he sighed at the routine of his life. He went back down stairs, took his cape from the clothes rack, put on his flat cap, and made his way into the kitchen, being careful to tread only on the newspapers neatly laid out before him.

'Cucumber sandwiches and a flask of tea,' his wife said, pointing to the haversack by the door.

'Thank you dear.' Once out into the backyard he checked the tyres and brakes of his bicycle, then tested his bell, a routine he had carried out for years.

Violet kissed him on the cheek, 'have a nice day.'

'Thank you dear.' He opened the backyard door and went out. Violet watched him free wheel down the street, waited a moment, then closed the door and returned to the kitchen to make a fresh pot of tea. Her crochet work was set out on the table. Violet was the champion crochet knitter of Barrow, and she even had an order from St. John's Church to make a cloth for the altar. She was the envy of her knitting circle.

There was a knock on the door. Annie Dodd stood outside waiting impatiently. 'Come on Violet,' she muttered to herself. Violet opened the door and her friend walked in. 'I just seen your Norman at the bottom of the street.'

'Yes,' replied his wife, 'he is going up to the lakes with the cycling club.'

'Oh!' A long drawn-out sigh came from the visitor, as if in a 'I know something you don't' manner.

'What's wrong?' came an abrupt retort from Violet.

'Nothing dear.'

'The other ladies will be here soon. I've got the sandwiches ready and I'll put the tea on'

'Cucumber and cress again I suppose,' muttered Annie to herself.

'What was that?' Violet called.

'Nothing dear,' she called back

Norman waited round the corner for about five minutes and was about to set off when Rita Forshaw came out of her house. 'Thought you weren't coming.'

'Changed my mind but if you moan about my sandwiches again, that's it.'

'Silly old trout,' Nobby muttered under his breath. He was in no mood for any trouble today.

'You say something?' she shrilled at him.

'No dear. Oh! Sugar!' he swore. Round the corner came Annie Dodd, her head down in the wind. She walked straight past without appearing to notice them. Nobby gave a sigh of relief. 'Come on Rita, we are meeting with the rest of the group at Dalton castle in half an hour.'

At ten o'clock precisely, they joined forces with the other ten members of Barrow Wheelers Cycling Club.

'Right Nobby, what's the route today?' asked one of the men. 'Good morning Rita, with us again are you?' he continued, smirking at his companions.

Rita just huffed to herself and said nothing.

'Right chaps, gather round.' Nobby had his Ordnance map open in front of him. 'The route today,' he explained, 'is to Ulverston, Newby Bridge, then on to Bowness, Windermere, and Ambleside. Drinks at the *'Old England Hotel'* then on to

Grasmere. We shall then climb Wrynose pass, have lunch in a lay-by and come across Hard Knott pass, down through to Broughton, and back to Dalton. Is that fine with every one? Capes on then gentlemen, and lady,' he ordered, smiling at Rita, who returned a grimace for his pains. 'Yes, it's going to be one of those days,' Nobby thought to himself,

Travelling through the Market town of Ulverston, they passed the *Canal Tavern*, aptly named after the canal which, one hundred years earlier, had traversed from the town centre to the thriving coastal port about a mile away. High up on a hill to their right was a huge monument overlooking the whole of Morecambe bay. It had been built in the shape of a lighthouse, in memory of Admiral Sir John Barrow, a local seafarer.

Travelling on through Greenodd, another coastal village, they turned inland to Newby Bridge where Lake Windermere begins. A hundred yards after manouvering over the quaint, hump-back bridge close to the *Swan Hotel*, they turned sharp left towards the east side of the lake. Climbing up the long winding road they could see *'Lakeside'* below, from where the lake steamers set sail and dozens of rowing boats appear in the summer. Heads down, they peddled in formation, any pedestrian having to jump quickly out of the way. Arriving in Bowness, where a steamer was just departing for Ambleside, they stopped for a short rest.

Having completed the ten-mile cycle alongside the lake, they finally arrived in Ambleside, pulling up at the entrance to the bar of the *'Old England.'* Two waiters were outside collecting glasses from the courtyard tables, and one turning to the other. 'Here they are again, the last of the big spenders.'

His colleague laughed and went in.

Nobby followed them. 'Twelve orange juices please,' he

ordered.

'Yes sir, I'll bring them out to you in a moment.'

Nobby returned to his colleagues. 'Not be long, just pouring the drinks,' he explained. The wind had dropped completely. Coming into view, it's engines throbbing, the steamship *Tern* cut a wake through the mirror-like lake that reflected the surrounding hills and trees and the small cottages on the far side

'Your drinks sir.' The minerals were set down with a heavy crash on the table, waking the cyclists from the tranquillity of the scene. Half an hour later the waiter watched as they sped up the road and out of the village like a united pack of ants. He glanced down at the tray on the table; a sixpenny piece lay there. 'The last of the big spenders indeed,' he smiled. Picking up the coin, he spun it and walked back into the hotel.

'Any tips?' shouted his colleague.

'No,' he replied, with a grin of self-satisfaction.

They rode like demons through Grasmere, then, turning right through the narrow streets, started the long climb up Wrynose to the pass. Most club members gave up all thought of cycling, eventually leaving only Nobby and Rita. Then, with only a couple of hundred yards to reach the summit, Rita gave in. Dismounting her bike, she looked back and watched as the trail of exhausted companions made the way up to her. 'Purchasing those Sturmey-Archer gears was a godsend,' Nobby smugly thought to himself. He pulled into a lay-by and walked back out into the road to wait for his bedraggled friends to arrive. Rita Forshaw propped her bike alongside Norman's, opened her saddlebag, and removed the packed sandwiches. The other members of the party, sitting a little further away from them, proceeded to eat their own lunches, occasionally glancing over to the couple and giving each other the nudge as if to say, 'Derby and Joan are at it again.'

Norman offered Rita a sandwich and enquired, 'What have you got this week?'

'Don't worry,' she snapped, 'it's not bacon. I'll open them when we've finished yours.' Norman thought the better course of valour was to keep his own mouth shut. He stood up, stretched himself, then walked behind a large boulder.

'And just where are you going?' asked Rita.

'If you must know,' he whispered, 'I'm going to have a pee.'

Rita giggled.

Standing there, relieving himself, Norman idly drew a picture in the loose pile of dirt and shale with the stream of urine. As he stopped and buttoned up his trousers he saw something glinting in the sunlight. Picking up a twig, he broke the surface around the object and recognised it as a cygnet ring. It would have been a nice cygnet ring except it still had a hand attached to it.

'Jesus Christ,' he shouted.

A voice from the other side of the boulder called back, 'What's up, Nobby, trapped your best mate?' They all laughed, except Rita who sniffled back, 'Don't be crude.'

Nobby came from behind the boulder. 'Nobby! your face is white.' Rita stood up and went to look at what Nobby was staring at.

'Go back!' he ordered.

'What's up Nobby,' his friends noticing the pallor of his face and the choking of his voice.

'There's a body buried there,' he replied, pointing. Pulling himself together, his army persona coming into force, 'Keep back now. There's a body here and we have to report it.'

'It does not need all of us to be here. Sidney,' pointing at the youngest of the party, 'about half a mile down the hill is a house, they will have a phone. Ring Grasmere police and tell them we have found a body buried in the lay-by. Direct them to where we are.'

Young Sidney, recognising the authority in his elder's voice, immediately got on his bike and cycled away. The other members started to congregate round the grave. 'Keep back,' Nobby commanded, 'we must not disturb anything. If you want to leave, do so, and I will give your names to the police if they need them.'

'Good idea Nobby. I'm on nightshift tonight and I don't want any hold ups,' said one of the cyclists. The rest agreed, and left Nobby and Rita to wait for the police.

Forty-five minutes later the first police car arrived. Out stepped a large portly gentleman, accompanied by a younger man sporting a fine but elegant grey beard.

'Inspector Harold Haslam, and this is my assistant, DC. Beverley.'

Nobby introduced himself and Rita, as well as young Sidney who had made the phone call. A second car arrived carrying the county coroner.

'You were quick sir,' D.C. Beverley said, with some surprise.

' 'I was in Sawrey a couple of miles away when my office rang.' The coroner went to the grave and began to carefully remove the shale and rocks from the body. 'Well,' he remarked, 'looks like he's been covered with a parachute.' Removing the silk shroud, the corpse became exposed. 'It's a German, he has a German uniform on,' he said sternly.

'Must have baled out from a plane,' said Beverley.

'And buried himself,' inspector commented sarcastically.

'Look at the ring,' said Norman.

'Just an ordinary onyx ring,' replied the coroner.

'Look again.' Nobby bent down and swivelled the onyx setting. 'That's the square and compass of a freemason.'

'So what?' asked the younger detective.

'German military are not freemasons,' explained Norman. 'That bloke is British, I'd bet my life on it, and who buried him anyway?'

'Get the area cordoned off constable,' instructed the Inspector. Then, turning to the coroner, he asked, 'any idea how long he's been dead.'

'Not for certain until I've done a full test, but probably around a week.' As he spoke an ambulance pulled into the lay-by. 'I'll get him to Whitehaven morgue for an autopsy and have the results for you in the morning.'

Haslam turned to Norman and his friends, 'Give your names and addresses to my assistant, but I don't think we will be needing you again. Thanks for your help.'

Nobby went to his bike and threw the unfinished sandwiches

and flask back into a saddlebag. 'Come on then, lets get home.'

CHAPTER FORTY

Heather was full of the gaiety of summertime as she skipped along the road. 'Just going for a walk,' she shouted to her aunt.

'Well don't be long, its an early tea today,' her aunt called out.

About a mile down the road she stopped and looked over the bridge into the river Duddon, where fish were darting about into the shadows. As a car came down the hill towards her, she stood close to the bridge to let it pass. Noticing a strange aerial on its roof, she peered inside at the smiling young face behind the wheel. The car pulled up on the far side of the bridge and P.C. William Wordsworth got out, leaving his helmet on the passenger seat. As he walked towards her he smiled. 'Well hello young lady, you're a long way from nowhere.'

She looked sharply at the handsome constable. 'As a matter of fact, young man,' she retorted, 'I live just up the road at the next farm.'

'The Morgan's farm,' he retorted with a grin, 'Oh! I know, you must be the little girl who is staying with her aunt and uncle.'

'I am not a little girl,' she replied, breathing in so that her breasts shoved out as if to make the point. 'You are thinking of my brother who is only seven. I am sixteen years of age, and I do not think you are very much older.'

'Twenty, to be exact, today.'

Oh! She cried, 'it's my birthday today as well.'

'We have something in common then. I'm Bill Wordsworth, and, before you say it, no I am not related to the poet.'

Heather giggled, 'Well my name is Heather Wright and I am sixteen today. So, many happy returns to you.'

'And may happy returns to you,' he responded. Then, with a beaming smile, he took her hand and kissed it.

She blushed and tried to change the subject. 'What's that on the roof of your car?'

Bill turned to where she was pointing. 'A direction-finding aerial to find radio transmitters that are being illegally used.'

Again changing conversation, he asked, 'Are you going to be at the hound trail tomorrow?'

'Yes,' she replied, 'but,' indicating the start of the valley, 'we shall watch it from over there so we can see the hounds coming over the crag's. Will you be there?'

'Yes, but I will be following them from the Coniston side.'

'Why's that?'

'We'll be sweeping the hills, searching for strangers.' Bill did not to try to elaborate, and she did not enquire further, as she was becoming strangely attracted to this slim young policeman.

'Well,' she said resignedly, 'you must be very busy?'

'Yes, I must get back to the station.' He turned to go, then, looking over his shoulder, he shouted, 'see you tomorrow then.'

Heather waved back, 'I'll save you a sandwich. Bye.' As the young constable drove up the hill, she wondered if she should have told him about the man in the river? She laughed to herself; 'No, he might ask me what I was doing there,' and blushed at her own sillyness.

CHAPTER FORTY-ONE

About half an hour after his niece had left, Ray Morgan arrived back at the farm. 'Hello love, every thing all right?'

'Yes dear,' his wife answered.

'Where's David?'

'Out in the barn with the dogs.'

'I'll never get them rounding sheep if he keeps treating them as pets. They're working dogs.'

'Oh! Leave the boy be, he loves animals. Told me he wants to be a farmer when he grows up,' She looked at Ray, 'Tells me you are the best teacher and farmer in the world.'

'Smart lad that,' Ray grinned, swelling with pride. 'He's right as well.' He ducked as a pillow flew past his head.

'Big-Head,' she called.

'Where is our young lady?' he asked idly.

'Gone for a walk up to the fells, I think. Shouldn't be long; told her tea would be ready soon.'

Ray jumped out of the chair, at the same time pulling on his jacket. 'Hell,' he muttered.

'What's wrong love?' his wife asked, concerned at his demeanour.

'There is somebody on the mountain, possibly a German.'

'Oh!' Margaret gasped in horror, 'Oh! Ray, find her.'

Ray grabbed his shotgun and a handful of cartridges, his wife followed him to the door.

'She went down the lane first, towards the Duddon,' said Margaret, pointing in the general direction.

Ray set off at a brisk pace, and as he reached the main road, he saw a police car coming towards him.

Observing a man with a gun, Bill Wordsworth got out of the car, then, seeing the concern etched in Ray's face Bill asked, 'What's the matter Mr. Morgan?'

'It's our lass. She has gone up the fells and with that German on the loose ...'

'Say no more. Get in, I have just left her at the bridge. As they drove off, he turned to Ray, 'What's this about a German?'

'Didn't Thompson tell you?'

'No, nothing definite. For a long time we have been looking

for someone using an illegal transmitter, but no Germans have been mentioned.'

They arrived at the bridge and got out. 'There she is just going into the bracken on the fell.' They both shouted to her but she did not hear them.

Meanwhile, Horst Stelmach had come back out of the woods. He crossed the river then sat for a moment, trying to identify the place where he had left his tunic. As he started to climb up the hill, he thought his ears were deceiving him. He could hear someone singing. *'Somewhere over the rainbow, way up high, that's where my heart is, here in a lullaby.'*

Crawling through the bracken, he came to the clearing where he had left his coat. But there was this beautiful young Frauline, the green foliage surrounding her was higher than her head. He watched transfixed as she lay on the green velvet of the moss, allowing the sun to warm her body, and oblivious to her surroundings. Suddenly they both heard the shouts of 'Heather' being called repeatedly.

She jumped up, quickly composing herself, then shouted back, 'Here I am.'

Her uncle and Bill Wordsworth came over the rise and through the bracken. 'Thank God you are ok, I was worried sick.'

'But uncle, I often come here, it's my favourite spot.' Then, seeing Bill, she blushed.

'It's too dangerous at the moment, darling, you are going to have to stay off the hills for a while.'

The German edged his way back down through the bracken. Ensuring that it was safe, he re-crossed the river and went back to the plane. He did not tell his colleague of his near escape.

Richter looked up and said, 'don't forget, tonight you'll have to climb up to the mine for some more food and discuss our plans for escaping.'

'I will make a drink and then leave before dark,' he nodded back.

Bill Wordsworth dropped Heather and Ray off at the bottom of the lane, Ray's wife being there to greet them. 'You had me really worried you two.'

'It's all right now woman, where's the tea?'

'Come on the both of you.'

Turning as he walked past the barn Ray shouted, 'Come on David, leave them dogs alone. They'll be too tired to work tomorrow.'

Arriving back at the Police station, Bill asked his colleague, 'Has the Sarg. mentioned anything about a German in the hills?'

'No,' Basset answered, 'why?'

'No matter, I'm sure it will be sorted out tomorrow.' The phone rang and Bill picked it up. 'Broughton police, can I help you?' He listened for a while, nodded at the phone, and replaced the receiver.

'Who was that?' enquired Basset.

'Grasmere police for Thompson.'

'Well! What did they want?'

Bill sat down at the table for a moment, then, shaking himself from his thoughts, replied 'Oh, them! They have found a body wrapped in a parachute on Wrynose pass.'

'English or German,' asked Basset.

'He was in a German uniform, but appears to be English.'

They both looked at each other and shrugged their shoulders.

Basset replied nonchalantly, 'wonders never cease.'

CHAPTER FORTY-TWO

The phone rang. 'Good evening, the Duckworth residence,' came the responding voice, 'Whom may I say is calling sir?' The butler waited for the reply.

'I'll se if she is available; one moment sir,'

'Who is it Thomas?' Said Stella.

'Sir Hughlock, Ma-am.' Thomas handed the phone over to her.

'Hello Mark, lovely of you to call. She listened for a while, 'Yes that would be very nice, fine, fine,' she repeated, 'Eight o'clock at the High Cross, bye, see you later.'

Putting down the phone she returned to her room, her sultry black eyes gazed into the mirror as she slowly undressed. Her thoughts were of Mark and the evening before her. 'If only he knew!' she thought, as she silently sang *'How much I love him so!'* to herself. She started to do an erotic dance when there was a knock on the door. Snatching her dressing gown from the bed, she called 'Who is it,' her voice croaking as if caught in an illicit act.

'Only me, dear,' her mother answered.

'I'll be down in fifteen minutes,' Stella called back.

'All right dear.'

Stella heard the sound of her mother's walking stick tapping on the oak floor as she moved towards the stairs. She smiled to herself, and, with an unintentional cruelty of which she was immediately ashamed of, called 'I'll be down before you,' knowing the struggle her arthritic mother would have in descending the long winding staircase. Choosing a black chiffon dress to match her eyes and hair, she began to dress, her thoughts and dreams, as she put each item on, was of Mark's hands taking them off. 'Pull yourself together, young woman.' Glancing at the door, she cupped her hands to her mouth and giggled like a school girl. Having applied rouge to her lips, she did a quick twirl in front of the mirror. 'You'll do,' she told herself, as if in acceptance of an award. Jauntily she swung about, skipped along the hallway and down stairs. Her mother was struggling to seat herself in a large leather bound chair, and Stella went over to assist her.

Her Father, smoking his favourite pipe, looked up at her, 'My, you are done up like a dogs dinner. Who's the lucky man?'

'If you must know, nosey,' pointing her finger at her own, 'I'm dining with Mark at the High Cross.'

Sir Arthur stood up and, leaning across the fireplace, tapped out the ash of his pipe, sat down again, opened the tin of tobacco and started to refill the pipe. 'Darling, be careful. You know full well that Mark has not only recently lost his parents, but his wife and a child in her womb. Not only is he vulnerable, darling but so are you.'

Her father's voice was soft and gentle and she felt a little ashamed. 'Oh! Daddy, I know, and I promise I won't rush him into anything, we are just having a nice meal together and enjoying each other's company. Truly daddy.'

'Fine dear, I'm sure you know best.' he replied.

She bent over and kissed him on the cheek. 'Oh! you,' she held her nose, 'that pipe smells awful.'

They all laughed, removing the tension that was in their hearts.

'Have a lovely evening dear.' Her mother offered her cheek to her daughter who dutifully kissed it.

'Be back before the carriage turns into a pumpkin,' her father called.

Turning, she blew him a kiss as she skipped out of the room.

Stella arrived at the High Cross some twenty minutes later. She knew she was early but did not want to hang around the house in case she blurted out at some horrible moment a confession to her parents that she was indeed madly in love with Mark. She would have to be patient, possibly until this awful war was over.

After ordering a drink at the bar she gazed at the pictures on the lounge wall, one of which showed a number of schoolgirls in gym slips, *'Dowdales V Gosforth hockey match 1935.'* She looked again and spotted herself sitting next to the captain, Gwen Benest.

'Best game for years, they reckon.'

Stella turned in the direction of the comment.

'Well, I'll be blowed, Gwen Benest.'

'Rigby now. Married a hotelier of all things, met him in Jersey just before the war.'

'Sit down Gwen. Oh! It must be years since we lost touch.'

'Yes, my father sold his business in Whitehaven, and we bought a hotel in Jersey. He died a year ago, and mother died shortly after I got married, so things have been a bit traumatic. We had to leave Jersey, it's now occupied by the Germans, they came as we got out. Fortunately we had already sold up and were ready to move, when this hotel came available. Our relations in Gosforth told us about it, so we bought it. We shall have to get together and talk old times.'

'I'd love to,' replied Stella. 'I'm eager to hear about Mr. Rigby.' Just then, Mark entered the lounge. 'Here's my friend coming now, hang on, I'll introduce you.'

Gwen looked to where her former school friend was indicating and stood up. Before Stella could say anything, Gwen said, 'Why, Mark Hughlock, you have grown, and all dressed up in a uniform. You look gorgeous.'

Mark and Stella looked astounded; Mark was first to recover. 'Gwen,' he hesitated, 'Gwen, er, Benest?'

'You know each other?'

Gwen looked at Stella and smiled conspiratorially, 'Oh! Mark and I go back a long way.'

'Yes,' grimaced Mark, 'to when we were about ten years of

age. This woman followed Niall and me around like a lame sparrow, especially when her parents came to stay with us for a summer holiday. How is your family by the way?'

'They're both dead I'm afraid,' she answered.

'I'm sorry, Gwen.'

'That's ok! Look, I'll leave you two love birds to get on, I have some work to do.' Turning sharply on her heels, she made her way back to the office.

'Oh! I hope I didn't upset her,' he remarked rather ponderously.

'She'll be all right. How's your day been then?'

'Great. The work is going better than anticipated, the men are working a dream.'

A waiter brought in their menu.

'Are you hungry,' asked Mark, looking up.

'Yes, I could eat a horse.'

Mark beckoned the waiter back. 'Two horses, medium to well-done please.'

Stella laughed and called Mark a fool.

Without a twitch on his face, the waiter replied, 'Would that be on the hoof or without sir?'

Stella burst into a fit of giggles like a school-girl.

'Touché,' said Mark to the waiter, then continued, 'I'll have the trout, and,' looking at Stella … 'rump steak, medium rare,' she replied, still giggling.

It was eleven o'clock and they had parked in a small lay-by on 'Corney Fell' overlooking the ancient Druid stones. The evening air was warm enough to leave the roof of the MG down. Stella lay back on the car seat, 'It's been a wonderful evening Mark.' Across the fells they could see the peaks of Langdale Pike and Scarfell, and, high up in the sky, the twinkling lights of Ulpha. To their side the moonlight glimmered on the sea. Stella sighed in contentment, hoping it would never fade.

Leaning over her, Mark looked deep into her eyes. 'You know, your eyes are so dark that you could be mistaken for a highwayman ready to steal,' then hesitating, 'to steal my heart away.'

'Mark darling, I would dodge all the Bow Street Runners for just that moment.'

Mark bent his head and touched her lips with his, then parted for a moment before kissing her fully. Stella's back arched and she responded by putting her arms around his shoulders hoping that he would never stop.

'Oh! Mark, I know its wrong but I love you.'

'I love you too, but we have to be realistic. The war, your parents, the work on my estate, and all the problems of the world,' he said wearily.

'Darling,' touching his lips with her fingers, 'Time is all we need. One day at a time, there is no rush. Whenever you are ready I will be here for you.'

He kissed her again and they held each other in their arms, staring at the hills and fells towards Dow Crags and the Old Man of Coniston.

CHAPTER FORTY-THREE

Niall O'leary had done as Bauer ordered. After soaking the German's tunic in aniseed he had dragged it up the mountain. Reaching the summit, he replaced it with another bundle of rags doused in the same way. Leaving the lure on the trail he entered the mine. Horst Stelmach was waiting for him.

'Where's Richter?' asked Niall, peering into the gloom.

'Sprained his foot,' he replied, 'it should be all right by tomorrow.'

Niall shrugged his shoulders and thought, 'That's his problem. Here's some more food and dry clothing, and by the way,' throwing the little German his tunic, 'you lost this?'

'Shiesse, this smells.'

'It's the smell of heather from the hillside,' lied Niall, 'now listen to me. In two days a boat will be here to take you and Richter out to a submarine. You will be accompanied by Bauer and two others who will be the guests of the German Government.'

'Who are they?'

'Never you mind, that's all you need to know for now. Tonight you must stay here until at least eight o'clock in the morning, as there will be a lot of activity on the fell side. It would be too dangerous for you to go back now as the night mist is closing in and you'd get lost. You have dry clothes, some food, and you can light a fire from the ample amount of dry wood about, but don't make it to big or you will smoke yourself out.'

Niall took a small drink from the flask of coffee that he had brought, nodded farewell to the young man, and left the mine. Stooping to spread more aniseed on the lure, he then proceeded to drag it down to Coniston, Stopping about a quarter of a mile from the village, he checked that he wasn't being followed and entered a deserted shepherd's hut. After lighting a fire he took a drink of whisky from his hip flask and dozed off.

CHAPTER FORTY-FOUR

It was five thirty in the morning when Mara drove into Lord McGowan's estate and dropped off the first five hundred Pheasant chicks. Cliff Tomblin came out of the cottage.

'Morning Mara, where's your dog?'

'Bracken's at home, a bit of rheumatism in her back legs.'

'Aye, it affects us all in the end,' chuckled the old gamekeeper.

'Kick off at six thirty then?'

'Aye! About that,' said Mara, 'see you on the fell then.'

'Possibly on the other side. I'm having an early walk over the crags.

Cliff, can you do me a favour? If I collect your dog, Mitzy, will you bring my pick-up truck back over to Ulpha. We can then have a few drinks together and I'll bring you and the dog and the rest of the pheasants back.

'Sure thing Mara, no problem.'

Mara drove to the *Church Inn* and parked his wagon. He looked over towards the fells where a mist hung like a shroud. He shivered with an apprehension that today was not going to be as successful as many might have thought. He shook himself and, with his head held high, set off, taking in the scenery that had been his life for so many years.

Passing the shepherd's hut, unaware that Niall was still inside, he carried on up the fell. The smell of aniseed was still apparent to his nose and Mara pondered as to whether Niall has been a bit heavy handed with the lure. Reaching the summit, he thought he saw something move in a small gully over to his right. Intrigued, he went towards the aperture leading into the old but now deserted mine. Noticing that the grass around it was well flattened, he moved forward apprehensively. Taking a brass horseshoe from his waist belt, he approached the entrance. The corrugated door was lying some feet away. 'Could be the wind I suppose,' he thought, edging into the mine. Then he became aware of the smell of smoke.

'Is there any one there? Don't be afraid, I won't do you any harm.'

Mara was beginning to think that he had been stupid in entering the mine in the first place. Through the gloom he could see the outline of a table with a lamp and a small suitcase on it. He touched the lamp. 'Shit, it's hot.' Putting the horseshoe down on the table he lit the lamp, the glistening of the copper pyrites in the roof flickered in unison with the flame. Then he noticed a passageway.

'Come on, who's there?' probably some tramp he thought. 'Come on, don't fart about. Who's there?' Still there was no reply.

He gave the suitcase a shake. 'It could be explosives, but then if it is, I wouldn't be here now,' he chuckled, and chided himself for being a bloody fool. 'Well I'll be dammed,' he gasped, as he opened the case and saw a transmitter, the earphones neatly coiled on top, and a small leather-bound booklet, which he opened. 'My God, it's a German codebook. As he turned the pages he noticed repeat references to 'PEDDLAR.'

'For Gods sake son, what have you been up to?'

His heart began to despair. 'What the bloody hell have you been up to,' he repeated to himself in anguish. Suddenly there was a noise between himself and the entrance. He turned quickly, and instinctively ducked as a bullet hit the roof where his head had just been. Before his assailant could fire again, Mara picked up the horseshoe and threw it in a sweeping motion, then heard the yell of pain as the missile struck home. The German, his wrist broken, turned and ran out of the mine onto the open ground, just as yelping hounds came over the rise. Immediately he was surrounded, the hounds tugging at his clothes and jumping up at him. Shocked and in pain he tried to ward off the animals.

Mara picked up the pistol and ran after him. By now the dogs had moved away from the young man, as if under orders, and were well on their way down the hillside heading towards Seathwaite, their baying dying in the distance. An eerie silence came over the area. As Mara walked toward the

German, who was now lying still on the ground, he noticed a group of people coming out of the mist from the east. Leading the party were Niall and Bill Wordsworth, and, a few yards behind, some of the owners of the hounds.

Niall was the first to reach them. Trying to avoid looking towards the mine, he asked, with an incredulous look on his face, 'Dad, what are you doing up here? And who is this?' pointing at the still form.

Mara went over to the body, and was about to say the hounds attacked him, when he stopped and turned the German over. 'Jesus, the top of his head is missing, the poor bugger's been shot.'

Out from the mist a voice called, 'Got him then, did I?'

They looked in the direction from where the call came. 'What are you doing here?' Wordsworth asked.

Thompson nodded toward the body. 'We have suspected for some time that there was a spy somewhere in these hills, and that's why our direction-finding vans have been scanning the area over the last few days. We planned this hound trail, to see if we could drive this fellow out into the open.'

'Why did you shoot him then?' queried Wordsworth, pointing at the rifle in the policeman's hand.

'Had to, he might have shot you,' indicating the pistol that Mara was holding.

Thompson left them, walked into the mine, and returned with the Radio transmitter. 'There, what did I tell you.'

Mara noticed that he did not have the codebook. 'Anything else?' Mara asked.

'No. Why, should there be?' Both Thompson and Niall stared intently at Mara.

Mara decided that he should keep his mouth shut for now, 'but by God,' he muttered to himself, 'Niall will have some explaining to do later.'

Bill Wordsworth brought them all back to attention. 'This must be the guy who buried that other fellow on Wrynose pass.'

'What fellow, what are you taking about,' an edge of panic came over Thompson.

'Didn't get the chance to tell you this morning Sarg. Grasmere CID found a body yesterday afternoon, they are not sure if it's that of an English man or a foreigner. They have sent the fingerprints to London.'

Thompson felt the urge to be sick, but controlled himself, realising that the time was getting near for a fast exit. Taking charge again, he ordered Wordsworth and three of the local farmers who were standing around the body, to use the corrugated sheet as a stretcher and take him down to Seathwaite.'

Niall's father went back into the mine, whilst the bearers, made their way down the mountainside. As they passed near to a small wood to the right, Richter was observing them. He could see an arm dangling over the side of the stretcher and the shredded tunic, then, to his surprise, his former passenger, rifle in hand.

He edged back into the woods to where the plane was hidden. He didn't like Stelmach all that much, thought he was a little effeminate, but he was one of his crew. They had been together long enough to know one another for good or for bad.

He sat for a moment looking at the dead embers of the fire 'If that bastard's killed him, for what ever reason, I will kill him if its the last thing I do.'

As the bearers filed down the hill, the spectators and owners of the hounds were gathered together, some collecting there bets, others eating sandwiches and drinking from their flasks. Cliff Tomblin, grinning from ear to ear, had collected the cup and the five-pound prize money from Mark and Stella.

'Bless you Miss and you to sir,' he said, doffing his cap in mock Edwardian style. He looked up as the crowd began to move towards the incoming party. The gamekeeper gestured towards them, 'looks like someone's been hurt.'

Thompson was leading, followed by Niall and Mara, who had caught up with them. Then the four body carriers, and, about fifty yards behind, the farmers, who were walking in single file.

Mark went over to Thompson. 'What's happened sergeant?'

'We've caught the spy, afraid he was killed. Pulled a gun on Mr. O'Leary there, had to shoot him.'

'What makes you think he was the spy?'

'Found a transmitter in a nearby mine. He had been there for some time.'

Mark composed himself. 'Who shot him?'

'I did!' Thompson acknowledged.

'I suggest you take him down to the village hall then, until he can be collected. Will you then ring Inspector Moses?'

Thompson nodded his head in agreement. 'I will make the call from the vicarage.'

The body was put on the back of Mara's pick-up truck and deposited in the care of Reverend Young. The crowd followed on to the *Pheasant Inn* where, as was the usual custom, a reception had been laid on. It was well into the night before Mark turned to Stella, 'I've had enough, how about you?'

Stella agreed, 'Yes I need my sleep, we have visitors coming in the morning.'

As they were leaving, Thompson and Niall, were sitting in a corner talking. Mark commented, 'Thompson's getting very friendly with Peddlar, isn't he?'

Mara was with Cliff Tomblin at the other end of the bar. 'I'm off now, Cliff,' the old man said.

'Nay! I'm not leaving yet. Tell you what, Mara, I'll get a lift back with one of the lads, you bring the other pheasants round when you're ready.'

Mara nodded, and went over to Niall 'Need you back at the caravan. Now!' and walked out to the truck. He sat there for a few minutes until Niall joined him.

Irritated, Niall protested, 'Out of sorts tonight aren't you'

Mara said nothing, put the car into gear and Niall's head shot back in the seat as Mara accelerated rapidly.

CHAPTER FORTY-FIVE

Hans Richter pulled on one of the sweaters that had been given to him by Niall, and doused the campfire with a bucket of water. Checking his pistol, he put it into his waistband and set off through the woods. Coming across the remnants of the hound-trail party who were still walking down the road side, he joined them.

One of the party turned to him, 'Good day wasn't it?'

He nodded in acknowledgement, for, although he understood some English, it was not enough to make a long conversation. A farmer drove his truck along side and shouted, 'Lift to the pub anyone?' Richter joined the others in the back of the truck, but, when they arrived in the village, he held back whilst the rest made their way across the road to the pub. Then, after a few minutes when nobody was about, he peered through a window, drawing back quickly. Niall and Bauer were seated under the window with their backs to him. He would have loved a drink but had no money. He decided to wait, and sat down at a large table in the courtyard. As other tables became full, a man and his female companion approached him. Being in uniform, Richter took the man to be a policeman.

'Mind if we join you?' Richter shrugged his shoulders, He listened to the couple talking, when the girl said to her friend, 'I really must go now, uncle is in there drinking, and Aunt Margaret will be expecting me back'.

'Oh, Heather, can't you stay longer? I am just getting to know you, and besides,' looking sadly at his drink, 'I have only just bought this.'

The girl laughed. 'You prefer a pint of mild to my company then do you?' She got up and started to walk towards the road. 'Oh! Hang on then, I'll give you a lift back to the farm.' Putting his arm around the girl's waist, which, to his delight she did not object to, he guided her to the car, gallantly opening the door for her. She curtsied mockingly and got in.

Richter watched as they drove off, then, taking a sip of the almost full pint of beer left on the table, grimaced, 'warm beer.' As the pub began to empty, he leaned against the wall in the darkened recess. An elderly man walked out of the pub, slamming the door behind him, and got into a truck that was parked over the road. A few moments later, he was joined by a man that Richter knew as Peddlar. Seeing an opportunity, Richter ran across the road and jumped unnoticed into the back of the truck, which sped off in a hurry. Twenty minutes later the vehicle stopped and he heard the driver's door slam, then a moment later the sound of the other door closing. Peering over to side, he watched as Peddlar followed the older man down the hill towards a caravan. When they were far enough away, he clambered out of the vehicle and followed them into a courtyard of a building that reminded him of a French chateau. In the darkness he found a sheet of tarpaulin, and decided that this was as warm a place as he was going to get for the night.

As Mara opened the caravan door, he was met by Bracken, his tail wagging. 'Hello old son,' he said, patting the dog warmly. Niall followed in and sat down. No words were said, as silence seemed, to Mara, the most appropriate thing at the moment, but all the time his temper was on the boil. He got up and went outside again, picking up some dry kindling from under a small shelter. Within a few moments he had a good blaze going. Pulling a rocking chair towards the fire, he sat down, lit his pipe, and lay back, his temper waning. The caravan door opened and Niall came out. Finding a large log to sit on, he lit himself a cigarette. The crackling from the fire and the smell of the wood smoke was all that interrupted the silence of the night.

Niall was the first to speak. 'Well?'

A wall of silence met him.

'Well,' he repeated, 'are you going to tell me what's up?'

Mara tapped the burnt ash out of his pipe and began to refill it. 'How does treason suit you? Plain bloody treason!'

'What the hell are you talking about?' his son protested. 'Oh! Bugger, you in this mood, I'm going to bed.'

'Ubermitten zeiten bitte, Peddlar.'

Niall froze, and slowly turned to face his father.

'"Ubermitten zeiten bitte, Peddlar,' Mara snarled, repeating the words out slowly with all the venom he could muster. He reached into his pocket and flung the codebook across the fireplace into Niall's chest.

Niall stared down at the booklet, there was a despair in his voice. 'You know?'

'Jesus Christ man,' Mara yelled, 'if Thompson had found that book,' he threw up his own hands, 'you bloody fool, they can hang you for treason.' 'How in God's name did you get mixed up in this?' He looked at Niall,.'Do you, know? Do you know,' his father was beside himself in rage, 'twenty years ago that could have been me.' There was contempt for himself in his own voice. Suddenly he stopped, his eyes opened in awareness. 'It's your Grandfather, isn't it?' the words almost choking him.

'You and that bloody family, I should have seen it coming.'

By now Mara was walking around in a circle, berating the night air. 'How the hell did you get mixed up with them?'

'Don't blame the lad!'

Mara and Niall looked round. From out of the shadows came a well-built man wearing a black leather jerkin and a fedora hat. A look of incredulation came on Mara's face. 'Calliag. Calliag O'Leary.'

Calliag came forward and sat on the trunk that Niall had vacated.

'Sit down brother, I've come a long way to talk to you.'

'With a gun in your belt?' answered Mara.

'Sit down,' he repeated. 'Your father and your mother wish you well, as do your brothers,' getting the formalities out of the way.

'All my brothers?' smirked Mara, yet without any real rancour.

Calliag leaned forward, intent on making his point. 'Yes Mara, all your brothers.'

Mara looked back suspiciously, but didn't reply.

'Twenty years ago Mara, I would have killed you, if you were in my sights.'

'And what makes the difference now?'

'Shelagh.'

'What's she got to do with anything?' Mara queried.

'You remember the night before the raid on Rosslane docks?'

'Aye. What about it?'

'That night, when you left her in the alley, Kevin was waiting in the shadows and overheard you talking to her. He made two and two add up to five, and in his anger, beat, raped and buggered the lass.'

'Dear god,' Mara lamented.

Calliag went on. 'The night of the raid, Shelagh informed the Garda.'

Mara looked up.

'But that's not all. She took a rifle with her and shot Kevin off the dock wall. The soldiers shot me, and your brothers were captured at the gasworks. We got six years jail each.'

'And what about Shelagh,' Mara asked quietly.

'She died from cancer a few days ago.' 'Martin, for twenty years I have held a false hate against you, because I thought you had betrayed us.'

'Do you honestly believe I would do such a thing to my own family, or anyone else for that matter?' Mara threw the words at him.

'I guess it was my own hatred and bigotry, and knowing that only you and a couple of others were aware of the plan. That got me confused. I'm sorry Mara, it's a scar I have lived with all these years.'

'Fuck you Calliag, how dare you come here pontificating your soul. I buried my hate for all the indiscriminate bombings we did, years ago. Now you come here with my lad,' gesturing toward Niall, 'now a bloody traitor to his own people.'

'He's no traitor, he fights for our cause. He took an oath.'

'You bloody hypocrite,' shouted Mara, pointing at his brother. 'It's you who are Irish, not him. His mother, his sisters, his friends, his country,' hysteria appearing for a moment 'he is English, and will hang if caught.'

Quietly, Calliag got up and crossed over to Niall. 'Well then, we shall have to see he doesn't get caught.'

Mara resigned himself to the situation, put his hands up as if in surrender, and went into the caravan.

Carriag turned to his nephew. 'The lorry is up the hill behind yours, there is a carton for your friend in the back, and one for you on the front seat.'

As Niall walked up the path, Carriag took out a cigarette and lit it from an ember in the fire. Mara came back out of the caravan carrying a bottle of whiskey and three tumblers.

'The lad's gone up to the wagon, I doubt he'll be back for a long while.'

Mara shrugged his shoulders in a couldn't care less fashion. 'So dad has got him rapped up in the cause, has he?'

His brother nodded, and went on to relate Niall's time in Ireland and his courage on the trawler. They talked long into the night, until Carriag raised his hands above his heads and yawned. 'It's been a long day, and its going to be even longer tomorrow.'

Mara did not ask any questions. 'Use my bed,' he offered, 'I have to go and check the pheasant pens anyway.'

Carriag acknowledged his thanks by raising his whisky glass, smiled, and took the remainder of the whiskey with him into the home. A few minutes later, Mara went up the path towards the trucks. The windows of his pick up were steamed up and he was unable to see in. 'Just as well,' he thought. He went to the other truck in which Calliag had arrived, shining his torch through the window. Not seeing anything, he climbed into the back where he discovered a packing case hidden underneath a tarpaulin. Grabbing a crowbar that lay nearby, he broke into it. Inside were two haversacks. He took out the first one and opened it.

'The stupid sods.' In front of him lay four bundles of dynamite, each attached with primed detonators, batteries, and timers. He opened the other bundle and found the same. 'Damn it Niall, what am I to do with you?' He felt so low and ashamed. Pulling himself together he went back to his own truck and collected a toolbag then returned to Calliag's truck. It only took fifteen minutes to complete what he had to do, after which he replaced the tools and went down to inspect his pheasants.

Niall opened the door of Callaig's truck and stood back, his jaw stood open in surprise and disbelief.

'I've been waiting a long time.' Mary flung herself out of the vehicle and into his arms. They fell back, locked together; he could hardly breath as Mary smothered him in kisses.

'Hang on, hang on, let me get my breath. How did you get here? Before you tell me let's get somewhere warmer. Our truck has more room than yours.' Niall took hold of her hand and kissed her on her moist lips.

'Niall, hurry, make love to me,' she pleaded, lying back along the seat. Soon the windows of the vehicle were dripping with condensation, their bodies entwined in passion. Eventually Niall stopped, exhausted.

'Spoil sport,' she laughed.

'Crikey! Give me a minute to get my breath back. Why did you come hear Mary?' his manner changing to one of concern.

'I found out about the trip and smuggled myself aboard. We were half way here before I was discovered, by which time it was too late for them to do any thing about it.'

They lay there until the early ours of the morning, when they were awakened by the sound of a motor bike. Mary and Niall were still dressing themselves as Thompson parked in front of their truck. Niall got out.

The German, now in civilian clothes, walked to the back of the wagon. 'Where are the explosives?'

'In the other truck,' answered Niall.

'Who's she?'

'My girl from Ireland, she has come with my uncle.'

As Carriag came up the drive towards them, Niall did the introductions.

'This is the plan,' said Carriag. 'Niall and I are going to Barrow, you need to have the boat ready off the coast of Ravenglass,' pointing at a spot on the map that he had produced. 'High tide is eight o'clock this evening, so be there one hour before, there will be three other passengers, myself and the two Dutch Royals.'

'There will be four passengers.' They turned round. Mara, a

shotgun under his arm, looked at Niall, 'You are going back with them.'

'Oh yes, please.' Mary looked at Niall 'Come with us.'

'I agree son, your time is up here, and your father is right, there will be no rest for anyone once the Dutch are found missing.'

Tearful, Niall went up to his father, 'I am so sorry dad.'

Before the emotion could take hold of him, Mara, choking back his own heartache, replied 'Go son, just go.' He turned and walked away. A few yards down the track, the tears still mounting in his eyes, he stopped and, without turning, called, 'God be with you son.'

Bauer turned to Niall, 'We have two hours before light, we must get into the docks and plant the explosives on the cruiser slipways. The launch is at eleven-forty-five, but by seven-thirty the area will be crawling with people. We can make our escape with the seven o'clock shift change.'

'It will be cutting it fine,' replied Niall, but the entrance to the yard is near the slipways. We can go undercover as workers.'

Getting into their respective trucks they set off. Carriag's boat was berthed in St.Bees' harbour, under the pretext of needing engine repairs. If they left the harbour at six o'clock they'd have ample time to go the few mile down the coast.

CHAPTER FORTY-SIX

'Telegram, Inspector.'

Haslam swung his feet from the table in response to the knock on the door. 'Right Beverley, give it here.'

> *Body fingerprints that of Major Peter Thompson, Military intelligence. Awaiting, further information from them. Will inform you a.s.a.p. signed D.S. Dawes. Scotland Yard.*

'Our mystery man has been identified, but what was he doing up in the hills.'

'Perhaps that German chap they found on Coniston killed him,' Said Beverley.

'Maybe,' Haslam muttered to himself. 'Still, inform all police stations of the identity of our man. I don't think we'll tread on anyone's toes.'

Beverley left to do as he had been ordered.

Ida Sykes, the area post office driver, brought the Telegram into Broughton police station.

'Telegram for you.' she sang out.

PC John Basset came out of the kitchen, a cup of tea in his hand. 'Cuppa, Ida?'

'No thanks dear, I've' got some mail to take to the Ulpha Lodge.'

'I'm on my way up there now, I can take it for you if you like.'

'Oh! I don't know, it's Royal Mail.'

'Ida!' he came round the counter, 'I work for the Government, we are all on the same side,' patronising her by patting her on the back

'All right then, tea no sugar.'

Twenty minutes later Basset had shut the police station door and driven off.

At eleven in the morning, Niall and Bauer were seated in the *King Alfred Hotel*, on Walney Island, overlooking the channel that separated them from the two cruisers, *'Jamaica'* and *'Spartan,'* that lay next to each other on the slipways, ready for launching. They had placed their charges at the bows, centres and sterns of the wooden supports, each set to explode in forty-five minutes.

'It was criminal the way they had been allowed to walk around unchallenged,' Niall thought to himself in wry amusement.

The Landlord came over to them, placing two pints of mild on the table. 'Nice day for the launch.'

'Yes,' agreed Bauer, 'should go with a bang.'

'Here comes the kids.' The landlord pointed out of the window at the lines of school children walking up from Ocean Road School. They were allowed to watch every launch, though most would admit that they only came to watch the backwash wave, caused by the ships as they slithered into the water, sweep up the steep embankment and catch an unwary school child.

The men picked up their glasses and walked out onto the bowling green to give themselves a higher vantage point. From across the water they could hear the sound of heavy hammers knocking in the wedges that held the ships back. When the last wedge had been placed, speeches would begin, and the bottle of champagne would crash against the hull.

The sirens began to wail, and the cruisers started moving slowly down the slipways. Hans Bauer, Major to the German Reich, and 'Agent Prevocatuer,' raised his glass in mock farewell, waiting for the explosions. The ships picked up speed and the crowds began to cheer.

'Come on,' Bauer said to himself, 'come on,' a note of anxiousness coming to him. 'Come on.' The ships were halfway down and still no explosion. 'Come on,' he screamed within himself. The ships cleared the launch site and hit the sea, the children rushed to the barriers to await the backwash. The agent's face was as black as thunder.

'Bloody Irish bombers, they're duds. All this effort for bloody duds.' He looked at Niall, and would have killed him with his bare hands if he could. He put his half-finished pint on a table and walked out to the car park. Niall meekly followed. They got into the truck and Bauer looked at his watch.

'Drive up the coast, I want to be at the Castle for five o'clock.' Crossing over the Jubilee Bridge, they looked up the channel to where the barges were waiting to move the two cruisers to their berths.

'What a way to win a war.' His co-conspirator spoke with amazing self-control.

CHAPTER FORTY-SEVEN

PC Basset drove onto the forecourt of the Hughlock Manor, picking up the letters from the seat beside him. He got out of the car and walked over to the main door. He knew that Mark Hughlock wanted his mail to be left there, even though he had not yet moved in. Having posted them through the letterbox, Basset tried the door, which proved locked. He peered through the bay windows, unintentionally bending his knees with satisfaction, like a pantomime copper. Moving round to the back, he checked the tarpaulin covers over the wooden structures that Oliver Clark's men had built, then, as he turned to walk back to his car, he heard a muffled sound behind him. Before he could make a move he felt a heavy blow to the back of his head. He staggered forward, pawing at the air as if to steady himself, then crumpled to the floor as he was hit again. With supreme effort he endeavoured to rise again but was hit for the third time. He did not rise. He did not know he was dead.

Richter stood over the bloodied body of the young policeman, breathing heavy with the exertions of the murder. He glanced at the lead pipe in his hands and threw it far into the rhododendrons. Grabbing the corpse by its feet, he dragged it to where he had thrown the pipe, rolled it into the bushes, then made his way down to the caravan in the valley.

He edged round the caravan door and slowly opened it. He entered and, glancing around, saw the unmade bed, the empty whiskey bottle and the three glasses. Opening a cupboard he found some bread, cheese and tomatoes. Eating greedily, he continued with his search until he came across Mara's shotgun, a box of cartridges lying by the side. Sweating profusely, he loaded the gun and entered the kitchen, where he discovered two more bottles of whiskey. He opened one and poured himself a large drink. 'Prost!' he saluted himself in a mirror. Then sat down and waited.

CHAPTER FORTY-EIGHT

Bill Wordsworth arrived at the police station at the same time as the Reverend Young. He turned at the sound of the Vicar's call.

'Constable, can I have a word with you?'

'Certainly sir, come on in.'

'Well actually, it's the sergeant I should be speaking to, as it's rather delicate.'

'I'm sorry vicar, but I've no idea where he is. He seems to be disappearing a lot lately.'

'Constable,' he hesitated, 'Bill,' being more familiar with the boy he had known since childhood, 'the German you brought down to the village hall yesterday.'

'Yes vicar, what about it?'

The vicar hesitated again.

'Damn it vicar, spit it out.' Bill could have cut his own tongue out at his blasphemy. 'Sorry Vicar.'

But the local clergyman seemed to ignore his outburst. 'Look,

I know you have been friends of Niall for a long time.'

'Not really vicar,' this time making sure he was more polite. 'Niall is a fair bit older than me, he was in his last year at school when I joined.'

'Oh! Never mind.' He went on to explain. 'The German had this in his pocket, it fell out when the authorities came round to take him away.' The Vicar showed Bill a half-empty packet of cigarettes.

Bill looked at it. 'So what?'

'Read what is on the back.'

Bill turned the pack over. 'HERR PEDDLAR' was inscribed in a scrawling pencil, but still legible.

A feeling of detest and betrayal came over Bill. 'The bastard.' Pulling himself together, he replied, 'thank you Vicar, I will deal with this,' and without entering the station, walked back to his car and drove off in the direction of Ulpha, thus failing to hear the station phone ringing.

CHAPTER FORTY-NINE

'Jesus wept!' Haslam jumped out of his chair, at the same time calling for Beverley. 'Get your arse in here,' yanking the phone from its cradle as he bellowed into it 'Get me inspector, shit! What's his name?'

'Superintendent Moses sir.'

'What! Well find him, its imperative. Tell him to get to Broughton police station, it's a matter of national urgency, understand?' Haslam slammed down the phone then picked it up again, 'Get me Broughton police station.' He waited a moment, then, as soon as he heard it ringing, put the phone down again thoughtfully.

'Well?' asked Beverley, 'do I get to know what's going on?'

'Major Peter Thompson, is what is described as a first class twit, sent down to act as a Sergeant at Broughton Police Station. He was given two objectives, first to find out who is sending transmissions to a foreign power, namely Germany, and second, to assist in the safe evacuation of some Royal or other. A Sergeant Thompson, reported for duty just over a week ago.' He flung his pipe down on the desk. 'We have Germans in the hills, and now in our police force. Get the car, we are going to Broughton.'

Meanwhile, Bill Wordsworth drew up with a screech at the Hughlock residence. Storming down the hill to the caravan, he pounded on the door, 'O'Leary, O'Leary.' The drive had not subdued his anger. He took hold of the door handle and pulled it open. Facing him was a double-barrelled shot gun.

'Peddlar, don't be stupid,' he said as he put his hands over his head. 'Who are you? Another Kraut bastard?' The contempt in Bills voice evident.

'Walk back please,' Richter ordered in his broken English. 'Where is Bauer? I have no time to waste, and your friend,' gesticulating up the hill with the gun, 'is in no fit state to tell me anything.'

'I don't know any Bauer,' he said, warily looking in the direction the gun had pointed.

'The Police Sergeant, you fool.'

As if struck with a bolt of lightning, all the little suspicions, the wonderings about Thompson's activities in the hills, the subtle lapse of information, came to light. 'Thompson's a German? He asked, incredulously.

'He was to get me and my navigator to the sea,' Richter explained, shrugging his shoulders. 'Appears I have to do it myself, but first I wish to avenge my navigator.'

'Why,' asked Bill, for the moment looking as if he might have a go at his opponent.

'I'm sorry, policeman, I have no time to answer more questions, back up please.' His antagonist stood down from the caravan and raised the gun at Bill. 'I am sorry, but this is necessary.'

Bill turned his head away, then heard a loud gasp. He looked back at his assailant, a horseshoe was sticking out of his chest. The German had dropped the gun and was down on his knees. Mara and his dog were about thirty feet away. Mara walked over and bent over the stricken man. 'Murder comes easy to you, doesn't it?'

'Fortunes of war,' the dying pilot gasped.

'My friend is in the woods, near to where you brought the body of Horst. You will find my plane and the body of Max Riss my bomb-aimer, as you English call them. Please see we all get a good funeral.' He coughed as blood came to his throat. 'If you find the bastard Bauer, please kill him for little Horst and me.'

'Where are they, shouted Bill.'

'Can't here you son, he's dead. But I think I know were they are. Come on.'

CHAPTER FIFTY

Mark stood in the Baronial Hall of Ravenglass Castle, waiting for Stella to finish dressing. Sir Arthur poured him a large whisky.

'How is Lady Sylvia?' Mark asked politely, trying to make small talk.'

'Not too good, staying in bed this evening. Baines, the butler, will look after her while I'm at the Lodge tonight.' 'You know Mark, your father would be proud of you if you joined the freemasons, he was co-founder of Ulpha Lodge with me. There are many of your friends who would welcome you.'

Mark nodded. 'When the war is over I shall be able to give full time to it. I probably know the rituals better than you, the way father used to practice on both me and our dog Max.'

'Lovely dog that,' acknowledged Sir Arthur, ' Sandilands if I remember. Fine breed.'

'Yes,' replied Mark, 'sixteen years of worship that dog gave to me, it broke my heart when it died. What time are you leaving?'

'Any time now, just waiting for my guest,' pointing his pipe upstairs.

Out in the courtyard they heard the screech of tyres on the

gravel. 'Sounds like someone's in a hurry.' The main door in the hall burst open followed by a shout of pain. 'What the devil was that?' As he and Mark made their way towards the commotion, the hall door opened and Thompson and Niall stormed in.

'What's the meaning of this,' demanded Sir Arthur.

'Get back in, both of you, we are hear to collect your two guests, and if you interfere I will shoot you.' Thompson was carrying a Browning automatic in his hand.

'Niall, what an earth is going on?' asked Mark, whilst keeping his eye on the gun.

'Do as you're told Mark, there has been enough hurt for one day.'

Stella, on hearing the noise, was half way down the stairs before she was noticed. Thompson waved the gun in a beckoning fashion, 'Down here please young lady.'

'Would someone please explain,' the old man repeated.

'Sit down, all of you,' his voice even more menacing. 'Let me introduce myself, I am Major Adolph Bauer, German intelligence. I have already had one fiasco today and I do not mean to have a second. Now! Where are the Dutch Royal Family?'

From the top of the stairs a suave young man called down to them. I'm afraid you have made a rather ghastly mistake old boy.' The man began to descend the stairs to join the others, who were seated.

'You are?' Bauer said, trying to recall the face.

'Yes old boy, Duke of Kent at your,' he hesitated, 'well I

suppose I am at your service. What with you waving that contraption at everyone.'

Angrily Bauer snarled. 'Tell me now, where are the other two?'

'It's like this, old boy, rather a 'cock-up' on the government's part. It appears the Queen suffers from claustrophobia. Damn well won't go by submarine after all. She decided on staying at Sandringham until other transport could be arranged.'

The agent was beside himself in rage, and Niall could only watch with nervous caution. 'We have no time to, as you English say, piss about.'

'Oh! Language, old boy, ladies you know,' pointing at Stella.

'You, playboy. You are brother to the King, aren't you?'

'Yes.'

'You will do, you are coming with us.'

'Fraid I can't old boy, got a lodge meeting tonight and it is getting rather late.' The Duke began to rise.

'Sit down. No stand up.' He was almost apoplectic.

'Oh, do make up your mind, I will be doing this most of the night at the lodge, and it is so tiresome.'

Stella stifled a giggle.

'On your feet now.' Bauer's patience was finally at an end, 'you are coming with me now, or I will shoot you along with these others.'

'Now just a minute, Bauer,' Niall cried with alarm, 'you cannot murder these people.'

'I have no choice,' he replied, raising his pistol.

Niall dived at him and made a grab for the gun. As they twisted, Niall was struck with the butt, temporarily stunning him. Bauer raised the pistol and a shot rang out. The German looked around with a look of amazement and disbelief. He raised the pistol again and a second shot was fired. Bill Wordsworth stood there, a smoking double-barrelled shotgun in his hands, his face ashen with the horror of what he had been forced to do.

Mara came in from behind him and crossed over to the body. 'He's dead.' Picking up the gun he looked at his son. 'Get out now.'

Bill raised the shotgun to Niall. 'You are under arrest you bloody traitor, I'll see you hang for the murder of Basset.'

'I didn't kill Basset,' protested Mara's son.

'Go on son, go. Bill has no cartridges in the gun, and,' waving the pistol, 'I've got this.'

Niall turned to Mark. 'Mark I am so sorry, 'nodding at his at his former best friend.

'Go Peddlar, just go.' He could not disguise his contempt for his one time comrade. In the distance they could hear sound of police sirens. Niall went over to his father and looked at him, there were tears in their eyes. Without a word, be ran down the lane to the estuary, where the trawler was waiting.

'Damn you Man,' cried Bill.

'Son, let's just say you owe me one.'

By the time Haslam arrived, Broughton Police Station was filled to the brim with policemen. Superintendent Moses was waiting. 'Well, what's this urgent problem of National security then?'

'Your bloody Sergeant is a German.'

Moses' face went comatose. 'Oh! God, the Royal family.' He picked up the phone, 'Haverigg army camp.' Speaking quietly into the phone for about two minutes, he then turning to Haslam, and said, 'Follow me, and pray we are not to late.'

Alarm bells and sirens were ringing as the convoy joined forces at the gates of Ravenglass castle. A young policeman ran out. 'Quick, down to the beach, they are getting away in a trawler.'

The army truck managed to travel about four hundred yards before getting hemmed in on the narrow track By the time they arrived at the beach it was too late, the boat was at least a thousand yards away, sailing its way through the tidal ebb into the moonlit horizon. Mark and Stella came up to the cliff edge and, holding each other, watched the distant lights fade away. Mara stood a few yards to one side, lit his pipe and turned away. For a few seconds they all looked away from the night-light, as if a curtain had been drawn across a theatre stage.

Mary and Niall stood at the stern of the boat, watching the coastline slip away. 'When we get back to Ireland, we shall make a new life together.'

Mary looked with sympathy at his tear glistened face. 'You will see your father again one day darling.'

His uncle came out of the wheel house, 'Niall, signal for you.'

Niall went into the radio room and listened.

Deep down below in the ocean, U-boat Captain Dieter

Morgeil watched as his radio operator sent out the coded message.

Gypsy King to Peddlar, do you read? He repeated the message several times and waited.

Peddlar to Gypsy King, reading you.

Gypsy King to Peddlar, have you had a good catch?

Peddlar to Gypsy King. All nets lost. Catch lost along with captain.

Gypsy King to Peddlar. Voyage a failure then?

Peddlar to Gypsy Kin., Voyage Negative, over and out.

Captain Morgeil picked up the written orders before him then read them again. Steady at periscope depth, he waited whilst the clear night sky came into view.

'Range?'

'One thousand yards, captain.'

'Number one torpedo ready?'

'Ready,' Captain.

He looked again at the trawler before him. 'Fire one,' he waited a moment and watched as the wake of the torpedo disappeared from view.

'Time to target, two minutes, captain.'

The sky filled with a short but bright glow.

'Down periscope, course due North. I will be in my cabin when needed.'

Nobby Pearce sat in front of the blazing brazier looking at the two stripes on his arm. 'No justice' he said aloud, as if telling the stars. 'One stripe off for shooting at a plane without authority. He opened his sandwiches that his wife had put up for him. Stale cucumber. 'Oh blimey, they're Rita's from my saddle bag.' He opened the other package, 'Bacon, bloody bacon. No Justice at all.'

THE END.

Barrow in Furness, a small town. The characters in our story, well, some are fact and some are fiction. Nobby Clark was indeed one of the finest rifle shots in the NorthWest and he and his wife were staunch supporters of the Rifle league.

The houses and the people mentioned all existed, but names have been changed to save embarrassment. Mara is based on a true life character who was bailiff and river warden at Ravenglass.

The 'Seraph' became a famous submarine, known for its many subterfuge activities. For example it was used for the disposing of a body off the coast of Spain, in what became known as 'The man who never was.'

The rest, well who knows, fact is, after all, fact. What is fiction? Barrow went on to make tankers, destroyers, aircraft-carriers, and nuclear submarines. It's people never bowed to tyranny, indeed two German planes were shot down from ack-ack and small arms fire on the very day mentioned, the whereabouts of the crash is not certain. The Duke of Kent died some two years later in an air crash.

HEARTS OF OAK WERE OUR MEN
AND WOMEN.

James Rigby